Enid Blyton

The Mystery of
the Hidden House

Also by Enid Blyton in Dean

The Mystery of the Burnt Cottage
The Mystery of the Disappearing Cat
The Mystery of the Secret Room
The Mystery of the Spiteful Letters
The Mystery of the Missing Necklace
The Mystery of the Pantomine Cat
The Mystery of the Invisible Thief
The Mystery of the Vanished Prince
The Mystery of the Strange Bundle
The Mystery of Holly Lane
The Mystery of Tally Ho Cottage
The Mystery of the Missing Man
The Mystery of the Strange Messages
The Mystery of Banshee Towers

First Term at Malory Towers
Second Form at Malory Towers
Third Year at Malory Towers
Upper Fourth at Malory Towers
In the Fifth at Malory Towers
Last Term at Malory Towers

Enid Blyton

The Mystery of
the Hidden House

First published in Great Britain 1948
Reissued 2009 by Dean
an imprint of Egmont UK Limited
239 Kensington High Street, London W8 6SA

ENID BLYTON ® Copyright © 1948
Chorion Rights Limited.
All rights reserved.

ISBN 978 0 6035 6432 1

1 3 5 7 9 10 8 6 4 2

Printed and bound in Singapore

Contents

1. THE BOY AT THE STATION

'It's today that Fatty's coming back,' said Bets to Pip. 'I'm so glad.'

'That's the sixth time you've said that in the last hour,' said Pip. 'Can't you think of something else to say?'

'No I can't,' said Bets. 'I keep on feeling so glad that we shall soon see Fatty.' She went to the window and looked out. 'Oh Pip – here come Larry and Daisy up the drive. I expect they will come to the station to meet Fatty too.'

'Of course they will,' said Pip. 'And I bet old Buster will turn up as well! Fancy Fatty going away without Buster-dog!'

Larry and Daisy walked into Pip's playroom. 'Hello, hello!' said Larry, flinging his coat on a chair. 'Won't it be nice when Fatty's back? Nothing ever seems to happen unless he's around.'

'We aren't even the Five Find-Outers without

him,' said Bets. 'Only four – and nothing to find out!'

Larry, Daisy, Fatty, Pip and Bets called themselves the Five Find-Outers (and Dog, because of Buster). They had been very good at solving all kinds of peculiar mysteries in the various holidays when they came back from boarding-school. Mr Goon, the village policeman, had done his best to solve them too, but somehow the Five Find-Outers always got a little ahead of him, and he found this very annoying indeed.

'Perhaps some mystery will turn up when Fatty comes,' said Pip. 'He's the kind of person that things always happen to. He just can't help it.'

'Fancy him being away over Christmas!' said Daisy. 'It was strange not having Fatty here. I've kept him his presents.'

'So have I,' said Bets. 'I made him a notebook with his full name on the cover in beautiful lettering. Look, here it is – Frederick Algernon Trotteville. Won't he be pleased?'

'I don't think he will,' said Pip. 'You've got it all dirty and messy, carrying it about.'

'I bought him this,' said Daisy, and she fished a box out of her pocket. She opened it and brought out a neat little black beard. 'It's to help him in his disguise.'

'It's a lovely one,' said Pip fingering it, and then putting it on his chin. 'How do I look?'

'Rather silly,' said Bets, at once. 'You look like a boy with a beard – but if Fatty wore it he would look like an elderly man at once. He knows how to screw up his face and bend his shoulders and all that.'

'Yes – he's really most clever at disguises,' said Daisy. 'Do you remember how he dressed up as Napoleon Bonaparte in the waxwork show last hols?'

They all laughed as they remembered Fatty standing solemnly among the waxworks, as still as they were, looking exactly like one.

'That was a super mystery we solved last hols,' said Pip. 'I hope one turns up these hols too. Anyone seen Mr Goon lately?'

'Yes, I saw him riding his bicycle yesterday,' said Bets. 'I was just crossing the road when he came round the corner. He almost knocked me down.'

'What did he say? Clear orf?' said Pip, with a grin.

Clear-Orf was the nickname that the children gave to Mr Goon the policeman, because he always shouted that when he saw them or Buster, Fatty's dog.

'He just scowled like this,' said Bets, and screwed up her face so fiercely that everyone laughed.

Just then Mrs Hilton, Pip's mother, put her head around the door. 'Aren't you going to the station to meet Frederick?' she said. 'The train is almost due!'

'Gosh! Yes, look at the time!' cried Larry, and they all sprang to their feet. 'He'll be there before we are if we don't hurry.'

Pip and Bets dragged on coats, and the four of them went thundering down the stairs like a herd of elephants. Crash, went the front door, and Mrs Hilton saw them racing down the drive at top speed.

They got to the station just as the train was pulling in. Bets was terribly excited. She hopped about first on one foot then on the other, waiting for Fatty's head to pop out of a carriage window. But it didn't.

The train stopped. Doors were flung open. People jumped down to the platform, some with bags that porters hurried to take. But there was no sign of Fatty.

'Where is he?' said Bets, looking upset.

'Perhaps he's in one of his disguises, just to test us,' said Larry suddenly. 'I bet that's it! He's dressed himself up and we've got to see if we can spot him. Quick, look round and see which of the passengers he is.'

'Not that man, he's too tall. Not that boy, he's not tall enough. Not that girl, because we know her. Not those two women, they're friends of mother's. And there's Miss Tremble. It's not her. Golly, which person can he be?'

Bets suddenly nudged Larry. 'Larry, look – *there's* Fatty! See that boy over there, pulling a suitcase out of the very last carriage.'

Everyone stared at the red-faced boy at the end of the train. 'Yes! That's old Fatty! Not such a good disguise as usual though – I mean, we can easily spot him this time.'

'I know! Let's pretend we *haven't* spotted him!' said Daisy suddenly. 'He'll be so disgusted with us. We'll let him walk right by us without saying a word to him. And then we'll walk behind him up the station slope and call to him.'

'Yes – we'll do that,' said Larry. 'Here he comes. Now – pretend not to know it's Fatty, everyone!'

So when the boy walked down the platform towards them, carrying his bag, and a mackintosh over his arm, the others didn't even smile at him. They looked right through him and beyond him, though Bets badly wanted to run up and take his arm. She was very fond of Fatty.

The boy took no notice of them at all. He marched on, his big boots making a clattering noise on the stone platform. He handed in his ticket at the barrier. Then he stopped outside the station, put down his bag, took out a red-spotted handkerchief and blew his nose very loudly.

'That's how Mr Goon blows his!' whispered Bets in delight. 'Isn't Fatty clever! He's waiting for us to go up to him now. Let's not! We'll walk close behind him, and when we get out into the lane, we'll call to him.'

The boy put his handkerchief away, picked up his bag and set off. The four children followed closely. The boy heard their feet and looked back over his shoulder. He scowled. He put down his bag at the top of the slope to rest his arm.

The four children promptly stopped too. When the boy picked up his bag and walked on again, Larry and the others followed at his heels once more.

The boy looked back again. He turned round and

said, 'What's the big idea? Think you're my shadows, or somethink?'

Nobody said anything. They were a little taken aback. Fatty looked so spiteful as he spoke. 'You clear orf,' said the boy, swinging round again and going on his way. 'I don't want a pack of silly kids following me all day long.'

'He's better than ever!' whispered Daisy, as the four of them walked on at the boy's heels. 'He quite scared me for a minute!'

'Let's tell him we know him,' said Pip. 'Come on! We can help carry his bag then!'

'Hey! Fatty!' called Larry.

'Fatty! We came to meet you!' cried Bets and caught hold of his arm.

'Hello Fatty! Have a good Christmas?' said Daisy and Pip together.

The boy swung round again. He put down his bag. 'Now, look here, who do you think you're calling Fatty? Downright rude you are. If you don't clear orf straight away, I'll tell my uncle about you. And he's a policeman, see?'

Bets laughed. 'Oh, Fatty! Stop being somebody else. We know it's you. Look, I've got a notebook for your Christmas present. I made it myself.'

Looking rather dazed, the boy took it. He glanced round at the four children. 'What's all this, that's what I want to know!' he said. 'Following me round – calling me names – you're all potty!'

'Oh Fatty, *please* be yourself,' begged Bets. 'It's a great disguise, it really is – but honestly we knew you at once. As soon as you got out of the train, we all said, "That's Fatty!"'

'Do you know what I do to people who call me names?' said the boy, looking round fiercely. 'I fight them! Anyone like to take me on?'

'Don't be silly, Fatty,' said Larry, with a laugh. 'You're going on too long. Come on, let's go and find Buster, I bet he'll be pleased to see you. I thought he'd be at the station to meet you with your mother.'

He linked the boy's arm in his, but was shaken off roughly. 'You're potty,' said the boy again, and he picked up his bag and walked off haughtily. To the surprise of the others, he took the wrong road. The way he went led to the village, not to his mother's house.

They stared after him, shaken and puzzled. A little doubt crept into their minds. They followed the boy at a good distance, watched him go to the village and then, to their enormous surprise, he turned in at the gate of the little house where Mr Goon, the policeman, lived.

As he turned, he saw the four children at a distance. He shook his fist at them and went to knock at the door. It opened and he went in.

'It *must* be Fatty,' said Pip. 'That's exactly the way he would shake his fist. He's playing some very deep trick on us indeed. Gosh – what's he doing going to Mr Goon's house?'

'He's probably playing a trick on Mr Goon too,' said Larry. 'All the same – I feel a bit puzzled. We didn't get even a wink from him.'

They stood watching Mr Goon's house for a little while and then turned to go back. They hadn't gone very far before there was a delighted barking, and a little black dog flung himself on them, licking, jumping and barking as if he had suddenly gone mad.

'Why, it's Buster!' said Bets. 'Hello Buster! You've just missed Fatty. What a pity!'

A lady was coming down the road, and they all smiled at her. It was Fatty's mother, Mrs Trotteville.

She smiled back at the four children.

'I thought you must be somewhere about when Buster suddenly tore off at sixty miles an hour,' she said. 'I'm going to meet Frederick at the station. Are you coming too?'

'We've already *met* him,' said Larry in surprise. 'He was in a really good disguise, Mrs Trotteville. But we spotted him at once. He's gone to Mr Goon's house.'

'To Mr *Goon's* house,' said Mrs Trotteville, in amazement. 'But whatever for? He telephoned me to say he had just missed the train, but was getting one fifteen minutes later. Did he catch the first one then? Oh dear, I wish he wouldn't start putting on disguises and things – and I *do* hope you won't all begin getting mixed up in something horrid as soon as Frederick comes home. *Why* has he gone to Mr Goon? Surely something odd hasn't turned up already?'

This was an idea. The children stared at one another. Then they heard the sound of a train. 'I must go,' said Mrs Trotteville. 'If Frederick isn't on that train, after phoning me that he'd missed the other, I shall be very angry indeed!'

And into the station she went, with all the children following.

2. HELLO FATTY!

The train drew in. People leapt out – and Bets suddenly gave a shriek that made everyone jump in fright.

'There *is* Fatty! Look, look! And he isn't in disguise either. Fatty! Fatty!'

Fatty swung little Bets off the ground as she and Buster flung themselves on him. He grinned all over his good-natured face. He kissed his mother and beamed at everyone. 'Nice of you to come and meet me. Gosh, Buster, you've made a hole in my trousers. Stop it!'

Mrs Trotteville was very pleased to see Fatty, but she looked extremely puzzled. 'The children said they had already met you once – in some disguise or other,' she said.

Fatty was astonished. He turned to Larry. 'What do you mean? I haven't arrived till now!'

The four children looked very foolish. They

remembered all they had said to the other boy. Was it possible that it hadn't been Fatty after all? – well, it couldn't have been, of course, because here *was* Fatty arriving on the next train. He couldn't possibly be on two trains at once.

'We've made complete idiots of ourselves,' said Larry, going red. 'You see . . .'

'Do you mind walking out of the station before the porters think we are waiting for the next train?' said Mrs Trotteville. 'We're the last people on the platform as it is.'

'Come on,' said Fatty, and he and Larry set off with his bag between them. 'We can talk as we go.'

Bets took his mackintosh, Pip took a smaller bag and Daisy took a bag of magazines. They were all extremely glad to see the real Fatty, to hear his determined voice, and see his broad grin.

'You see,' began Larry again, 'we didn't know you'd missed the first train so we came down to meet you – and we thought you might be in disguise – so when a big boy got off the train, we thought he was you!'

'And we didn't say anything at first, just to puzzle you, so we thought,' said Pip. 'We followed this boy out of the station and he was really fed up with us.'

'And then we called to him and said, "Fatty!" ' said Bets. 'And you see, he *was* big – and he swung round and said he fought people who called him rude names.'

'I wonder he didn't set on you all!' said Fatty. 'You might have known I wouldn't say things like that to you, even if I *was* disguised. Where does he live?'

'He went to Mr Goon's house,' said Daisy. 'He said Old Clear-Orf was his uncle.'

'Gosh! You've put your foot in it properly!' said Fatty. 'Goon *has* got a nephew – and I bet he's asked if he can stay with him. Won't he be mad when he knows how you greeted him!'

'It's a great pity,' said Mrs Trotteville, who had been listening to all this with astonishment and dismay. 'He must have thought you were very rude. Now Mr Goon will probably complain about the behaviour of you children again.'

'But Mummy – can't you see that . . .' began Fatty.

'Don't begin to argue, please Frederick,' said Mrs Trotteville. 'It seems to me that you will have to go and explain to Mr Goon that the others thought his nephew was you.'

'Yes Mummy,' said Fatty in a meek voice.

'I do want you to keep out of any mysteries or trouble these holidays,' said Mrs Trotteville.

'Yes Mummy,' said Fatty. Mrs Trotteville heard a suppressed giggle from Bets and Daisy. They knew perfectly well that Fatty didn't mean a word he was saying. Who could keep him out of a mystery if he even so much as smelt one? Who could imagine that he would go and explain anything to Mr Goon?

'Don't say "Yes Mummy," and "No Mummy," like that unless you mean it,' said Mrs Trotteville, wishing she didn't feel annoyed with Fatty almost as soon as she had met him.

'No Mummy. I mean, yes Mummy,' said Fatty. 'Well – I mean whatever you want me to say, Mummy. Can the others come for tea?'

'Certainly not,' said Mrs Trotteville. 'I want to have a little chat with you and hear all your news – and then you have your bag to unpack – and soon your dad will be home, and . . .'

'Yes Mummy,' said Fatty hastily. 'Well, can the others come round afterwards? I haven't seen them at all these hols. I've got presents for them. I didn't send them any at Christmas.'

The mention of presents suddenly made Bets remember that she had given her precious notebook to the other boy. She bit her lip in horror. Oh no! He had put it into his pocket! She hadn't asked for it back because she had been so scared when he had offered to fight them all, that she had forgotten all about the notebook.

'I gave that boy the present I made for you,' she said in a rather shaky voice. 'It was a notebook with your name on the front.'

'Just what I want!' said Fatty cheerfully, and gave Bets a squeeze. 'I'll get it back from that boy, don't you worry!'

'Now, just remember what I said,' warned Mrs Trotteville, as they came to her gate. 'There's to be no silly feud with that boy. He might be very nice.'

Everyone looked doubtful. They were as certain as they could be that any nephew of Mr Goon's must be as awful as the policeman himself. Buster barked loudly, and Bets felt sure he was agreeing with them in his doggy language.

'Mummy, you haven't said if the others can come round this evening,' said Fatty, as they went in at the gate.

'No. Not this evening,' said Mrs Trotteville, much to everyone's disappointment. 'You can meet them tomorrow. Good-bye children. Give my love to your mothers.'

Fatty and Buster disappeared up the path with Mrs Trotteville. The others outside the gate looked gloomily at one another and then walked slowly down the road.

'She might have let us have just a *little* chat with Fatty,' said Larry.

'We made an awful noise last time we went to Fatty's,' said Bets, remembering. 'We thought Mrs Trotteville was out, do you remember? – and played a dreadful game Fatty made up, called Elephant Hunting . . .'

'And Mrs Trotteville was in all the time and we never even heard her yelling at us to stop because we were making such a row,' said Pip. 'That was a good game. We must remember that.'

Well, do you think that boy *was* Mr Goon's nephew?' said Daisy. 'If he tells Mr Goon what we did, we'll get a few more black marks from him!'

'He'll know who we are,' said Bets dolefully. 'That boy's got the notebook I made – and there's Fatty's name on it. And, oh dear, inside I've printed in my best handwriting, headings to some of the pages. I've printed CLUES, SUSPECTS, and other things like that. So Mr Goon will know we're looking out for another mystery.

'Well, silly, what does that matter?' demanded Pip. 'Let him think what he likes!'

'She's always so scared of Old Clear-Orf,' said Daisy. 'I'm not! We're much cleverer than he is. We've solved mysteries that he hasn't even been able to *begin* solving.'

'I hope Mr Goon won't come and complain to our parents about our behaviour to that boy,' said Pip. 'Honestly, we must have seemed a bit mad to him. Mr Goon will probably think we did it all on purpose – made a fool of the boy just because he was his nephew.'

Pip's fear of being complained about was very real. He had strict parents who had very strong ideas about good and bad behaviour. Larry and Daisy's parents were not so strict and Fatty's rarely bothered about him, as long as he was polite and well-mannered.

But Pip had had some angry tellings-off from his

father, and he and Bets were always afraid of Mr Goon coming to complain. So, when they arrived home that afternoon for tea, they were horrified to hear from their maid, Lorna, that Mr Goon had rung up their mother ten minutes before.

'I hope you haven't got into mischief,' said Lorna, who liked the children. 'He says he's coming to see your Ma tonight. She's out for tea now. I thought I'd just warn you in case you've gone and got yourselves into trouble.'

'Thank-you Lorna,' said Pip and went to have a gloomy tea in the playroom alone with Bets, who also looked extremely down in the dumps. How *could* they have thought that boy was Fatty? Now that she came to think of it, Bets could quite clearly see that the boy was coarse and lumpish – not even Fatty could look like that!

The two children decided to warn Larry and Daisy, so they rang them up.

'Gosh!' said Larry. 'Fancy listening to tales from that idiot of a nephew about us! I don't expect my mother will pay much attention to Mr Goon – but yours will! Horrid old man. Cheer up. We'll meet tomorrow and discuss it all.'

Pip and Bets waited for their mother to come in. Thank goodness their father was not with her. They went down to greet her.

'Mummy,' said Pip, 'We – er – we want to tell you something. Er – you see . . .'

'*Now*, what mischief have you got into?' said Mrs Hilton impatiently. 'Have you broken something? Tell me without all this humming and hawing.'

'No. We haven't broken anything,' said Bets. 'But you see, we went to meet Fatty at the station . . .'

'And there was a boy that we thought was Fatty in one of his disguises,' went on Pip, 'so we followed him up the road, pretending not to know him . . .'

'And then we called out "Fatty" to him, and told him we knew him – and he was angry, and . . .'

'And what you mean is you made a silly mistake and called a strange boy "Fatty", and he was annoyed,' said Mrs Hilton, making an impatient tapping noise on the table. 'Why *must* you do idiotic things? Well, I suppose you apologised, so there's not much harm done.'

'We didn't actually apologise,' said Pip. 'We really thought he *was* Fatty. But he wasn't. He was Mr Goon's nephew.'

Mrs Hilton looked really annoyed. 'And now I suppose I shall have that policeman here complaining about you again. Well, you know what your father said last time, Pip – he said . . .'

The door opened and Lorna came in. 'Please Madam, there's Mr Goon wanting to see you. Shall I show him in?'

Before Mrs Hilton could say yes or no, the two children had opened the French windows that led to the garden and had shot out into the darkness. Pip wished he hadn't gone as soon as he was out there, but Bets clutched him so desperately that he had shot off with her. A great draught of icy air blew into the sitting-room behind them.

Mrs Hilton closed the garden door, looking cross. Mr Goon came into the room, walking slowly and pompously. He thought Mr and Mrs Hilton were proper parents – they listened to him seriously when he made complaints. Well, he was going to enjoy himself now.

'Sit down, Mr Goon,' said Mrs Hilton, trying to be polite. 'What can I do for you?'

3. ERN

Pip and Bets went round to the kitchen door and let themselves in. The cook was out and Lorna was upstairs. They fled past the big black cat on the hearth rug and went up to their playroom.

'I should have stayed,' said Pip. 'I haven't done anything wrong. It was silly to run away. It will make Mummy think we really are in the wrong.'

'Listen! Isn't that Daddy coming in?' said Bets. 'Yes, it is. He'll walk straight in on top of them, and hear everything too!'

Mr Goon seemed to stay a long time, but at last he went. Mrs Hilton called to Pip.

'Pip! Bring Bets down here please. We have something to say to you.'

The two children went downstairs, Bets quite plainly scared, and Pip putting on a very brave face. To their surprise, their parents did not seem angry at all.

'Pip,' said his mother, 'Mr Goon came to tell us that he has his nephew staying with him. He says he is a very nice lad indeed, very straightforward and honest – and he says he would be glad if none of you five led him into trouble. You know that every holidays you seem to have been mixed up in mysteries of some kind or other – there was that burnt cottage – and the disappearing cat – and . . .'

'And the spiteful letters, and the secret room, and the missing necklace,' said Pip, relieved to find that apparently Mr Goon hadn't done much complaining.

'Yes. Quite,' said his father. 'Well, Mr Goon doesn't want his nephew mixed up in anything like that. He says he has promised the boy's mother to look after him well these holidays, and he doesn't want you dragging him into any mystery or danger . . .'

'As if we'd *want* to do that!' said Pip, in disgust. 'His nephew is just a great clod. We don't want to drag him into anything – we'd like to leave him severely alone.'

'Well, see you do,' said his mother. 'Be friendly and polite to him, please. Apparently you were very rude and puzzling to him today – but as Pip had already explained to me the mistake you made, I saw that you didn't really mean to be rude. Mr Goon was very nice about that.'

'We won't drag his nephew into anything,' said Pip. 'If we find a mystery, we'll keep it to ourselves.'

'That's another thing I want to say to you,' said his father. 'I don't like you being mixed up in these things. It is the job of the police to solve these mysteries and to clear up any crimes that are committed. It's time you five children kept out of them. I forbid you to try and solve any mysteries these holidays.'

Pip and Bets stared at him in the greatest dismay. 'But – we belong to the Five Find-Outers,' stammered Pip. 'We *must* do our bit if a mystery comes along, I mean, really . . . why, we couldn't possibly promise to . . .'

'Mr Goon has already been to see Larry and Daisy's parents,' said Mrs Hilton. 'They have said that they too will forbid their children to get mixed up in any mysteries these holidays. Neither you nor they are to look for any, you understand?'

'But – but suppose one comes – and we're mixed up in it without knowing?' asked Bets. 'Like the missing necklace mystery.'

'Oh, one won't come if you don't look for it,' said Mr Hilton. 'Naturally if you got plunged into the middle of one without your knowledge, nobody could blame you – but these things don't happen like that. I just simply forbid you to look for any mystery these holidays, and I forbid you above all to allow Mr Goon's nephew to get mixed up in anything of the kind.'

'You can go now,' said Mrs Hilton. 'Don't look so miserable! Anyone would think you couldn't be happy without some kind of mystery round the corner!'

'Well,' began Pip, and then decided to say no more. How could he explain the delight of smelling out a mystery, of making a list of clues and suspects, of trying to fit everything together like a jigsaw puzzle till the answer came and the picture was complete?

He and Bets went out of the room and climbed up the stairs to their playroom. 'Fancy Larry and Daisy being forbidden too,' said Pip. 'I wonder if Mr Goon went to Fatty's parents too?'

'Well, I shouldn't think it would be any good forbidding Fatty to get mixed up in anything,' said Bets.

Bets was right. It wasn't any good. Fatty talked his

mother and father over to his point of view under the very nose of Mr Goon.

'I've been very useful indeed to Inspector Jenks,' he told his parents. 'You know I have. And you know I'm going to be the finest detective in the world when I'm grown up. I'm sure if you ring up the Inspector, Mummy, he will tell you not to forbid me to do anything I want to. He trusts me.'

Inspector Jenks was a great friend of the children's. He was chief of the police in the next town, head of the whole district. Mr Goon was in great awe of him. The children had certainly helped the Inspector many times in the way they had tackled various mysterious happenings.

'You ring up the Inspector, Mummy' said Fatty, seeing that the policeman didn't want Mrs Trotteville to do this at all. 'I'm sure he'll say Mr Goon is wrong.'

'Don't you bother the Inspector, Mrs Trotteville, please,' said Mr Goon. 'He's a busy man. I wouldn't have come to you if it hadn't have been for this young nephew of mine – nice fellow he is, simple and innocent – and I don't want him led into all sorts of dangers, see?'

'Well, I'm sure Frederick will promise not to lead him into danger,' said Mrs Trotteville. 'It's the last thing he would want.'

Fatty said nothing. He was making no promises. He had a kind of feeling that it would be good for Mr Goon's nephew to be led into something if he was as simple and innocent as the policeman made out. Anyway, all this was just to make sure that the Five Find-Outers didn't solve another mystery before Mr Goon did! Fatty could see through *that* all right!

Mr Goon, not feeling very satisfied, departed ponderously down the garden path, annoyed to find that his bicycle had suddenly developed a puncture in the front tyre. It couldn't possibly have been anything to do with that boy, who had been in the room the whole time – but Mr Goon thought it was a very funny thing the way unpleasant things happened to him when he was up against Frederick Algernon Trotteville!

The Five Find-Outers met at Fatty's the next day. Buster gave everyone a hilarious welcome. 'Now!' he barked, 'we are all together again. That's what I like best.'

But four of them, at least, looked gloomy. 'That spoilsport of a Goon,' said Larry. 'We were just waiting for you to come home and find another mystery to solve, Fatty. Now we're forbidden even to look for one.'

'All because of that goofy nephew of Mr Goon's,' said Daisy.

'Well – *I'm* going to do exactly as I've always done,' said Fatty. 'Look out for a mystery, find my clues and suspects, fit the pieces together – and solve the whole thing before Mr Goon even knows there's anything going on. And I'll tell you exactly what I'm doing the whole time!'

'Yes – but we want to *share* it,' said Pip. 'Share it properly, I mean – not just look on while you do it all. That's no fun.'

'Well, I don't suppose anything will turn up these hols at all,' grinned Fatty. 'Can't expect something *every* time, you know. But it would be rather fun to pretend we're on to something and get Mr Goon's nephew all hot and bothered about it, wouldn't it? He'd say something to Mr Goon, who wouldn't know whether to believe it or not – and he'd get into a mighty stew, too.'

'That's a wizard idea,' said Larry, pleased. 'Really wizard. If we can't find a mystery ourselves, we'll make up one for that boy. That'll serve Mr Goon right for trying to spoil our fun!'

'Let's go and see if we can find the boy,' said Fatty. 'I'd be interested to see what sort of a fellow you mistook for me in disguise! Must be jolly good-looking, that's all I can say!'

They all went to the village. They were lucky because just as they came in sight of Mr Goon's house, his nephew came out, wheeling his uncle's bicycle, having been ordered by Mr Goon to take it to the garage and get the puncture mended.

'There he is!' said Bets excitedly. Fatty looked and an expression of deep disgust came over his face. He gazed at the Find-Outers in disappointment.

'Well! *How* you could think that boy was me – even in *disguise*, I really don't know! He's an oaf! A clod! A lump! Not a brain in his head. Good gracious, surely I don't look in the *least* like him?'

Fatty looked so hurt that Bets put her arm in his and squeezed it. 'Fatty! Don't be upset. We thought it was one of your clever disguises.'

The boy wheeled his bicycle towards them. He

stopped when he saw them, and to their surprise he grinned.

'Hello! I know all about your mistake yesterday. You made me all hot and bothered. I told my uncle and he spotted it was you. Said you called yourself the Find-Outers, or some such thing. He said you were a set of cheeky toads.'

'What's your name?' asked Pip.

'Ern,' said the boy.

'*Urn*?' said Bets in surprise, thinking of the great tea urns her mother had at mothers' meetings.

'SwatIsaid,' said Ern.

Nobody understood the last sentence at all. 'I beg your pardon? What did you say?' asked Larry politely.

'I said "SwatIsaid,"' said Ern impatiently.

'Oh – he means "It's what I said,"' explained Daisy to the others.

'Course it is – short for Ernest, see?' said Ern. 'I got two brothers. One's Sid, short for Sidney, the other's Perce, short for Percy. Ern, Sid and Perce – that's us.'

'Very nice,' murmured Fatty. 'Ern suits you marvellously.'

Ern looked pleased. 'And Fatty suits you,' he said, handsomely. 'Right down to the ground it does. And

Pip suits him too – bit of a pipsqueak, isn't he? Wants to grow a bit, I'd say.'

The Find-Outers thought these remarks were out of place from Ern. He was getting a bit too big for his boots.

'I hope you'll have a nice holiday with your uncle,' said Bets, suddenly very polite.

Ern made a curious chortling noise. 'Oooh! My uncle! His high-and-mighty-nibs! Says I mustn't get led into danger by you! Well, you see here – if you get hold of any mysteries, you just tell me, Ern Goon. I'd like to show my uncle I've got better brains than his.'

'That wouldn't be very difficult,' said Fatty. 'Well, Ern – we'll certainly lead you to any mysteries we find. I expect you know that your uncle has forbidden us to solve any ourselves these hols – so perhaps you could take our place and solve a mystery right under his nose?'

Ern's rather protruding eyes nearly fell out of his head. 'Jumping snakes! Do you mean that? Lovaduck!'

'Yes. We'll provide you with all sorts of clues,' said Fatty solemnly. 'But don't you go and tell your uncle in case he gets angry with us.'

'You bet I won't,' said Ern.

'Oh, Ern – can I have back that notebook I gave you by mistake yesterday?' said Bets suddenly. 'It wasn't meant for you, of course. It was meant for Fatty.'

'I was going to use it for my portry,' said Ern, looking disappointed. He took it out and held it for Bets to take. 'I love portry.'

'What's portry?' asked Bets, puzzled.

'Portry! Lovaduck, don't you know what's portry. It's when things rhyme, like.'

'Oh – you mean poetry,' said Bets.

'Swatlsaid,' said Ern. 'Well, I write portry.'

This was so astonishing that nobody said anything for a moment.

'What sort of poetry – er, I mean portry?' asked Fatty.

'I'll recite you some,' said Ern, looking very pleased with himself. 'This here one's called *The Pore Dead Pig*. He cleared his throat and began,

> *How sad to see thee, pore dead pig,*
> *When all . . .*

'Look out – here's your uncle!' Larry suddenly said,

as a large dark blue figure appeared in Mr Goon's little front garden. A roar came from him.

'What about my BIKE! Didn't I tell you I wanted it right back?'

'So long!' said Ern hurriedly, and shot off down the street at top speed. 'See you later!'

4. FATTY IS MYSTERIOUS

ERN soon became a terrible pain. He lay in wait for the Find-Outers every day, and pestered them to tell him if they had smelt out any mystery yet. He kept wanting to recite his 'portry'. He shocked the five children by his very low opinion of his uncle, Mr Goon.

'We've got a low opinion of Old Clear-Orf ourselves,' said Larry, 'but really, to hear Ern speak of his uncle, anyone would think he was the meanest, slyest, greediest, laziest policeman that ever lived!'

Ern was always telling dreadful tales about his uncle. 'He ate three eggs and all the bacon for his breakfast, and he didn't leave me nothing but a plate of porridge,' said Ern. 'No wonder he's bursting his uniform!'

'My uncle isn't half lazy,' he said another time. 'He's supposed to be on duty each afternoon, but he just puts his head back, shuts his eyes and snores till

33

teatime! Wouldn't I like the Inspector to come along and catch him!'

'My uncle says you all want locking up for a few days, you're just a set of cheeky toads,' said Ern, yet another time. 'He likes *your* mother and father, Pip – but he says Fatty's parents are just the . . .'

'Look here, Ern – you shouldn't repeat what your uncle says about us or our parents,' said Fatty. 'It's a rotten trick. You know full well that Mr Goon wouldn't tell you all these things if he thought you were going to repeat them.'

Ern gave one of his chortles. 'Lovaduck! What do you suppose he says them for? Course he wants me to tell you them! Nice easy way for him to be rude to you.'

'Really?' said Fatty. 'Well, two can play at that game. You tell your uncle we think he's a . . .'

'Oh don't, Fatty,' said Bets, in alarm. 'He'll only come round and complain again.'

'He can't complain to *your* parents about what *I* say,' said Fatty.

'Oh yes, he can,' said Pip. 'You should just see him walking into our house like a flat-footed bullfrog, as pompous as a . . .'

Ern gave such a loud chortle that everyone jumped. Pip stopped in a hurry.

'That's a good one, that is!' said Ern. 'Lovaduck, I'd like to see Uncle Theophilus when I tell him that!'

'If you repeat that I'll fight you!' said Pip, furious with himself for saying such a silly thing in front of Ern. 'I'll knock your silly nose off, I'll . . .'

'Shut up, Pip,' said Fatty. 'You can't even box. You ought to learn boxing at school like I do. You should just see me box! Why, last term I fought a chap twice my size, and in five minutes I . . .'

'Had him flat on his back!' finished Larry, 'with a couple of black eyes and a squashed ear.'

Fatty looked surprised. 'How do you know?' he said. 'Have I told you before?'

'No, but your stories always end in some way like that,' grinned Larry.

'Found any mystery yet?' inquired Ern, who didn't like to be left out of the talk for long. Fatty at once looked secretive.

'Well,' he said, and hesitated. 'No, I don't think I'd better tell you, Ern. You'd only split to your uncle. You just can't keep your mouth shut.'

Ern began to look excited. 'Come on! You've got

something, I know you have. You said you'd tell me if you was on to a mystery. Lovaduck! Wouldn't it be a sell for Uncle if I got on to a mystery and solved it before he got a sniffofit.'

'What was that last word?' asked Fatty. Ern had a curious habit of running some of his words together. 'Sniffofit? What sort of a fit is that? Does your uncle go in for fits?'

'Sniffofit!' repeated Ern. 'Can't you understand plain English? Sniffofit.'

'He means "sniff of it,"' said Daisy.

'SwatIsaid,' said Ern, looking sulky.

'Swatesaid,' said Fatty at once to the others. They giggled. Ern scowled. He didn't like it when the others made fun of him. But he soon cheered up.

'Go on – you tell me about this mystery you've got,' he begged Fatty.

Fatty, of course, knew of no mystery at all. The holidays, in fact, stretched dull and dreary in front of him, with not a hint of any mystery anywhere. Only Ern promised a little fun and excitement. Fatty looked mysterious.

He began to speak in a whisper. 'Well,' he said, 'it's like this.' He stopped and looked over his shoulder as if there were people listening. Ern began to feel thrilled.

Then Fatty shook his head firmly. 'No, Ern. I can't tell you yet. I don't think I'd better. I'm only at the beginning of things. I'll wait till I know a little more.'

Ern could hardly contain his excitement. He clutched Fatty's arm. 'Look here, you've *got* to tell me!' he hissed. 'I won't breathe a word to Uncle. Go on, Fatty, be a sport.'

The others watched Fatty, trying not to laugh. They knew he hadn't anything to tell. Poor old Ern – he just swallowed everything he was told.

'I'll wait till I've a bit more to tell,' said Fatty. 'No, it's no good, Ern. Not even the others know anything yet. The time hasn't come yet to develop the case.'

'Lovaduck! That sounds good,' said Ern, impressed. 'All right, I'll wait. Do you think I ought to get a notebook and write in it the things young Bets here wrote in yours – the one she gave you for a present?'

'It wouldn't be a bad idea,' said Fatty. 'You've a notebook in your pocket, I see – bring it out and we'll show you what to write.'

'No. That's my portry notebook,' said Ern. 'Can't

write nothing in that except portry.' He took it out and flicked over the pages. 'Look – I wrote a pome last night – proper good pome it was too. It's called *The Pore Old Horse*. Shall I read it to you?'

'Well, no – not now,' said Fatty, looking at his watch and putting on a very startled expression. 'My goodness – look at the time. Sorry, old horse – pore old horse – but we can't stop today. Another time perhaps. Get a notebook, Ern, and we'll write in it all you ought to have in a proper mystery notebook.'

The five went off with Buster, grinning. Ern went back to his uncle pondering whether to repeat Pip's words to him – what were they now? Flat-footed bullfrog. That was good, that was. Good enough to put into a pome!

'Ern and his pomes and portry!' giggled Daisy. 'I wish I could get hold of that portry book – I'd write a poem in it that would make Old Clear-Orf sit up!'

'Quite an idea!' said Fatty, and put it away in his mind for future use. 'Now Find-Outers, we'd better plan what sort of wild-goosechase we're to send Ern on! We can't possibly disappoint him. We've got to give him a bit of excitement.'

They went to Pip's playroom and began to plan. 'It

wouldn't be a bad idea to practise a few disguises,' said Fatty thoughtfully. 'It doesn't look as if we're going to have much fun these hols, so we might as well make our own.'

'Oh, yes – *do* let's practise disguises,' said Bets, thrilled.

'We're going to have a good time with old Ern,' chuckled Fatty. 'Now, let's plan. Anybody got any ideas?'

'Well – what about a mystery kidnapping or something like that?' said Larry. 'Men who kidnap rich men's children and keep them prisoner. We might get Ern to try and rescue them.'

'Or we might have mysterious lights at night flashing somewhere, and send Ern to see what they are,' said Bets.

'Go on. We're getting some good ideas,' said Fatty.

'Or what about a robbery – with the loot hidden somewhere – and Ern has to find it?' suggested Daisy.

'Or a collection of clues to puzzle Ern. You know how we once put a whole lot of clues down for Clear-Orf,' said Pip. 'My word – I'll never forget that.'

Everyone laughed. Fatty tapped his knee thoughtfully with his pencil. 'Really good ideas, all of them,' he said. 'Super, in fact. I vote we try and use all of them. Might as well give Ern good measure. And if old Mr Goon gets excited about it too, so much the better. I bet Ern won't be able to keep it dark. Mr Goon will know there's something up – but he won't know how much is pretence and how much isn't. We'll have them both on a string!'

'It won't be as good as a real mystery, but it will be great fun!' said Bets, hugging herself. 'It will serve Mr Goon right for coming to complain to Daddy and Mummy! And for trying to do *us* out of a mystery these hols.'

'Not that there's even a shadow of one at the moment,' said Daisy.

'Well, now, let's get down to it,' said Fatty. 'Ern will come complete with his notebook next time we see him, I'm sure of that. We'll put down the usual heading – Clues, Suspects, Progress, and so on. Then we'll begin providing a few clues. We'd better let him find them. He'll be really happy if he thinks he's better at spotting things than we are. I'll make up some kind of story, which I won't tell you now, so that it will seem quite fresh to you. You can listen with large eyes and bated breath!'

'What's bated breath?' asked Bets. 'Do we breathe fast, or something?'

'No – we just hold it, silly,' said Pip. 'And don't you go and give the game away, Bets. It would be just like you to do that!'

'It would *not*,' said Bets indignantly. 'Would it, Fatty?'

'No. You're a very good little Find-Outer,' said Fatty, comfortingly. 'I bet you'll bate your breath better than anyone. Hello, what's that?'

'Our dinner is ready,' said Pip gloomily. 'It always comes when we're in the middle of something.'

'Spitty,' said Fatty, and got up.

'What do you mean – *spitty*?' said Larry.

'He means "It's a pity!" ' said Bets with a giggle.

'SwatIsaid,' said Fatty, and got ready to go.

5. IN FATTY'S SHED

The next day, Ern got a message that filled him with excitement. It was a note from Fatty.

> *Developments. Must talk to you. Bottom of my garden, twelve o'clock.*
> *F.T.*

Mr Goon saw Ern goggling over this note and became suspicious at once. 'Who's that from?'

'One of my friends,' said Ern haughtily, and put it into his pocket.

Mr Goon went a purple red. 'You show it to me,' he said.

'Can't,' said Ern. 'It's private.'

'What do you mean – *private*!' snorted Mr Goon. 'A kid like you don't know what private means. You give me that note.'

'But Uncle – it's only from Fatty to say he wants

to see me,' protested Ern.

'You show that note to me!' shouted Mr Goon and Ern, scared, passed it over. Mr Goon snorted again as he read it.

'Gah! All a lot of tommy-rot! Developments indeed! What does he mean by that?'

Ern didn't know, and he said so several times, but his uncle didn't believe him. 'If that there cheeky toad is up to his tricks again, I'll skin him!' said Mr Goon. 'And you tell him that, see?'

'Oh, I will, Uncle,' said Ern, trying to edge out of the room. 'I always tell them what you say. They like to hear. But it's not right of Pip to say you're a flat-footed bullfrog, I did tell him that.'

Before the purple Mr Goon could find his tongue to say what he thought of this, Ern was out of the house and away. He mopped his forehead. Lovaduck – his uncle was a hot-tempered chap all right. Anyway, he hadn't forbidden him to go; that was something!

He arrived at the bottom of Fatty's garden and heard voices in the shed there. It was Fatty's workroom and playroom. He had made it very comfortable indeed. On this cold winter's day, he had a stove burning brightly and the inside of the shed was warm and cosy. A tiger-skin was on the floor, old and moth-eaten but looking very grand, and a crocodile skin was stretched along one side of the shed wall. The Five Find-Outers were eating roast chestnuts. They had a tin of condensed milk and were each having a dip in it with a spoon as they talked.

Ern looked in at the window. Ha! They were all there. Good! He knocked at the door.

'Come in!' called Fatty, and Ern went in. An icy draught at once came in with him.

'Shut the door,' said Daisy. 'Oooh! What a draught. Hello, Ern. Did you enjoy your egg for breakfast?'

Ern looked surprised. 'Yes. But how did you know I had an egg for breakfast?'

'Oh – we're doing a bit of detecting for practice this morning,' said Daisy. The others tried not to laugh. Ern had spilt a good bit of his egg down the front of his jacket at breakfast, so it was not a difficult bit of detecting!

'Sorry you had to leave in such a hurry to come here,' said Fatty, solemnly.

Ern looked even more surprised. 'Lovaduck! Is

that another bit of detecting? How'd you know I left in a hurry?'

Ern had no coat, so *that* wasn't a very difficult bit of detecting either. Nobody explained to Ern how they knew about his breakfast or his hurry, and he sat down feeling rather puzzled.

'Perhaps you'd like to tell me what *I* had for breakfast,' said Fatty to Ern. 'Go on – do a bit of detecting too.'

Ern looked at Fatty's solemn face, but no ideas about breakfast came into his mind. He shook his head. 'No. I can see this sort of thing wants a lot of practice. Coo, I wasn't half-excited when I got your note this morning. My uncle saw me reading it.'

'Did he really?' said Fatty with interest. 'Did he say anything?'

'Oh, he got into a rage, you know, but I soon settled *that*,' said Ern. 'I just told him what I thought of him. "Uncle," I said, "this is a private note. It's none of your business, so keep out of it." Just like that.'

Everyone looked at him admiringly but disbelievingly. 'And what did he say to that?' asked Pip.

'He began to go purple,' said Ern, 'and I said,

"Now calm yourself, Uncle, or you'll go pop. And don't go poking your nose into what I do with my friends. It's private." And then I walked out and came here.'

'Most admirable!' said Fatty. 'Sit down on the tiger-skin rug, Ern. Don't be afraid of the head and the teeth. He's not as fierce now as he was when I shot him in the Tippylooloo Plain.'

Ern's eyes nearly fell out of his head. 'Lovaduck! You been tiger-shooting? What about that thing up on the wall? Did you shoot that too?'

'That's a crocodile skin,' said Bets, enjoying herself. 'Let me see, Fatty – was that the third or fourth crocodile you shot?'

Ern's respect for Fatty went up a hundredfold. He gazed about him with the greatest awe. He looked at the fierce head of the tiger rug, and felt a bit scared of it, even though it was no longer alive. He moved a little way from the snarling teeth.

'You said in your note there were developments,' said Ern eagerly. 'Are you going to tell us anything today?'

'Yes. The time has come for us to ask you to do something,' said Fatty, in a solemn voice that sent a

46

thrill down Ern's spine. 'I am uncovering a very mysterious mystery.'

'Coo,' said Ern, in a hushed voice. 'Do the others know?'

'Not yet,' said Fatty. 'Now listen all of you. There are strange lights flashing at night over on Christmas Hill!'

'Oooh,' said Ern. 'Have you seen them?'

'There are rival gangs there,' said Fatty, in a grave voice. 'One is a kidnapping gang. One is a gang of robbers. Soon they will get busy.'

Ern's mouth fell open. The others, although they knew it was all Fatty's make-believe, couldn't help feeling a bit thrilled too. Ern swallowed once or twice. Talk about a mystery! This was a whacker!

'Now the thing is – can we get going, and find out who they are and their plans, before they start their robbing and kidnapping?' said Fatty.

'*We* can't,' said Bets, in a dismal voice. 'We've been forbidden to get mixed up in any mystery these hols.'

'So have we,' said Larry and Daisy together. 'Yes, it's bad luck,' said Fatty. 'I'm the only one who can do anything – but I can't do it alone. That's why I've

47

got you here this morning, Ern. You must help me.'

Ern took in all this rather slowly, but with the utmost excitement and delight. He swelled out his chest proudly.

'You can count on me,' he said, and made his voice deep and solemn. 'Ern's with you! Coo! I feel all funny-like. I bet I'd write a good pome with this sort of feeling inside me!'

'Yes. It could begin like this,' said Fatty, who could reel off silly verse by the mile.

> *There's a mystery a-moving*
> *Away on Christmas Hill,*
> *Where kidnappers and robbers*
> *Are waiting for the kill.*
> *But when kidnappers are napping*
> *And robbers are asleep,*
> *We'll pounce on them together*
> *And knock them in a heap!*

Everyone laughed. No one could reel off verse like Fatty. Ern gaped and couldn't find a word to say. Why, that was wonderful portry! To think Fatty could say it all off like that!

He found his voice at last. 'Lovaduck! Did you make all that up out of your head just this minute? It takes me hours to think of a pome – and even when I do, it won't rhyme for ages. You must be one of them weird things – a genius.'

'Well – you never know,' said Fatty, trying to look modest. 'I remember having to write a poem – er, I mean, pome – for class one day, and forgetting all about it till the master pounced on me and asked for mine. I looked in my desk, but of course it wasn't there because I had forgotten to write one. So I just said, "Sorry, sir, it seems to be mislaid – but I'll recite it if you like." And I stood up and recited six verses straight off out of my head. What's more, I got top marks for it.'

'I don't believe you,' said Pip.

'Well, I'll recite it for you now if you like,' said Fatty indignantly, but the others wouldn't let him.

'Stop boasting,' said Larry. 'Let's get down to work. How did we get on to this poem business anyway? You'll have Ern wanting to recite next!'

Ern would have been only too willing to oblige, but most unfortunately, in his hurried departure from his uncle's house, he had left his portry notebook – a very grand one with black covers and an elastic band, and a pencil down the back.

'Mr Goon's got one like that,' said Bets. 'Did he give you that?'

Mr Goon would not even have dreamed of giving his nephew one of his precious notebooks, provided for him by the Inspector. Ern licked the end of the pencil and looked round triumphantly. 'Give it me! I should think not! I pinched it out of his drawer.'

There was a horrified silence. 'Then you'll jolly well give it back,' said Fatty. 'Or *you'll* be pinched one day. You're disgusting, Ern.'

Ern looked hurt and astonished. 'Well, he's my uncle, isn't he? It won't hurt him to let me have one of his notebooks – and I'm going detecting, aren't I? You're very high-and-mighty all of a sudden.'

'You can think us high-and-mighty if you like,' said Fatty, getting up. 'But we think *you're* very low-down to take something out of your uncle's drawer without asking him.'

'I'll put it back,' said Ern, in a small voice. 'I wouldn't have taken it for my portry – but for detecting, well, somehow I thought that was different. I kind of thought I *ought* to have it.'

'Well, you think again,' said Fatty. 'And put it back before you get into trouble. Look – here's a notebook of mine you can have. It's an old one. We'll tell you what to write in it. But mind – you put that black one back as soon as you get home!'

'Yes, I will Fatty,' said Ern humbly. He took the old notebook Fatty held out to him, and felt about in his pocket for a pencil, for he did not feel he dare use the one in the black notebook now. Fatty might get all high-and-mighty again.

'Now,' said Fatty, 'keep this page for clues. Write the word down – Clues.'

'Clues,' said Ern solemnly, and wrote it down. The word 'Suspects' came next. 'Coo,' said Ern, 'do we have suspects too? What are they?'

'People who *might* be mixed up in the mystery,' said Fatty. 'You make a whole list of them, inquire into their goings-on, and then cross them off one by one when you find they're all right.'

Ern felt very important as he put down the things Fatty told him. He licked his stump of a pencil, and wrote most laboriously, with his tongue sticking out of the corner of his mouth all the time.

Buster suddenly growled and cocked up his ears.

Fatty put his hand on him. 'Quiet Buster,' he said. He winked at the others. 'I bet it's Old Clear-Orf snooping round,' he said. Ern looked alarmed.

'I wonder he dares to come snooping after Ern, considering the way he got ticked off by Ern himself this morning,' said Fatty innocently. 'If it *is* your uncle, Ern, you'd better send him off at once. Bit of cheek, tracking you down like this!'

Ern felt even more alarmed. A shadow fell across the cosy room, and the Find-Outers and Ern saw Mr Goon's head peering in at the window. He saw Ern with a notebook. Ern looked up with a scared face.

'You come on out, Ern,' boomed Mr Goon. 'I got a job for you to do!'

Ern got up and went to the door. He opened it and out shot Buster in delight. He flew for Mr Goon at once, barking madly.

'Clear orf!' yelled Mr Goon. 'Here you, call off your dog! Ern, hold him! He'll take a bite out of my ankle soon! Clear orf, you pestering dog!'

But it was Mr Goon who had to clear orf, with Buster barking at him all the way, and Ern following in delight. 'Go on, Buster!' he muttered under his breath. 'Keep it up! Good dog then. Good dog!'

6. ERN GETS INTO TROUBLE

The Five Find-Outers were very pleased with their little bit of work that morning. 'We'll keep Ern busy,' said Fatty. 'And as I'm pretty sure he'll let everything out to Mr Goon – or Mr Goon will probably dip into Ern's notebook – we shall keep *him* busy too!'

'It's a pity Mr Goon came and interrupted our talk this morning,' said Bets, getting up to go. 'We were just getting on nicely. Fatty, what's the first clue to be?'

'Well, I told Ern that this morning,' said Fatty. 'Mysterious lights flashing Christmas Hill at night! Ern will have to go and find out what they are.'

'Will you go with him?' asked Bets.

'No. I'll be flashing the lights,' said Fatty with a grin. The others looked at him enviously.

'Wish we could come too,' said Larry. 'It's maddening to be forbidden to do anything these hols.'

'Well, you're not forbidden to play a trick on

somebody,' said Fatty, considering the matter. 'You're forbidden to get mixed up in any mystery or to go and look for one. You're not looking for a mystery, and there certainly isn't one, so I don't see why you and Pip can't come.'

The others' faces brightened. But Bets and Daisy were soon disappointed. 'We won't take the girls,' went on Fatty. 'We'll have to find something else for them to do. Look here – I'll do a bit of disguising the first night Ern goes mystery hunting – and you two boys can do the light flashing. I'll let Ern discover me crouching in a ditch or something, so that he really will think he's happened on some robber or other.'

'Yes – that would be fine!' said Larry. 'When shall we do it?'

'Can't do it tonight,' said Fatty. 'We may not be able to get in touch with Ern in time. Tomorrow night, say?'

'Wasn't Ern funny when you spouted all that verse,' said Larry, with a grin. 'I don't know how you do it Fatty, really I don't. Ern thinks you're the world's wonder. I wonder if Sid and Perce are just as easy to take in as Ern. Are we going to meet again today?'

'If I can get my mother to say you can all come to tea, I'll telephone you,' said Fatty. 'I don't see why I can't go and buy a whole lot of cakes, and have you to tea down here in the shed. We'd be nice and cosy, and we could make as much noise as we liked.'

But alas for Fatty's plan, an aunt came to tea, and he was made to go and behave politely at teatime, handing bread and butter, jam and cakes over in a way that Ern would have admired tremendously.

Ern was not having a very good time with his uncle. He had tried in vain to replace the notebook he had taken, but Mr Goon always seemed to be hovering about. Ern didn't mean to let his uncle see him put it back!

He kept trying to go into his uncle's office, which was next to a little wash place off the hall. But every time he sauntered out into the hall, whistling softly as if he hadn't a care in the world, his uncle saw him.

'What you want?' he kept asking. 'Why are you so fidgety? Can't a man have forty winks in peace without you wandering about, and whistling a silly tune?'

'Sorry, Uncle,' said Ern meekly. 'I was just going to wash my hands.'

'What, *again*?' said Mr Goon disbelievingly. 'You've washed them twice since dinner already. What's this new idea of being clean? I've never known you wash your hands before unless I told you.'

'They feel sort of – sticky,' said Ern, rather feebly. He went back into the kitchen, where his uncle was sitting in his armchair, his coat unbuttoned, and his froggy eyes looking half-closed and sleepy. Why didn't he go to sleep as he usually did?

Ern sat down. He picked up a paper and pretended to read it. Mr Goon knew he was pretending, and he wondered what Ern was up to. He didn't want to wash his hands! No, he wanted to go into his uncle's office. What for? Mr Goon thought deeply about the matter.

A sudden thought came into his mind. Aha! It was that cheeky toad of a boy, Frederick Trotteville, who had put Ern up to snooping about his office to see if any mystery was afoot. The cheek! Well, let him catch Ern snooping in his desk, and Ern would be in trouble! He began to hope that Ern *would* do a bit of snooping. Mr Goon felt that he would quite like to give somebody a really good telling off! He was in that sort of mood, what with that dog snapping at his ankles and making him rush off like that in front of Ern.

He closed his eyes. He pretended to snore a little. Ern rose quietly and made for the door. He stopped in the hall and looked back. Mr Goon still snored, and his mouth was half-open. Ern felt he was safe.

He slipped into the office, and opened the drawer of the desk. He slid the notebook into the drawer – but before he could close it, a wrathful voice fell on his ears.

'Ho! So that's what you're doing – snooping and prying in my private papers! You wicked boy – my own nephew too, that ought to know better.'

'Uncle! I wasn't snooping! I swear I wasn't.'

'What were you doing then?' demanded Mr Goon.

Ern stood and stared at his uncle without a word to say. He couldn't possibly own up to having taken the notebook – so he couldn't say he was putting it back! 'What are you snooping for? Did that cheeky toad of a boy tell you to hunt in my desk to see what sort of a case I was working on now? Did he tell you to find out any of my clues and give them to him?' said Mr Goon angrily.

'No, Uncle, no,' said Ern, beginning to blubber

in fright. 'I wouldn't do that, not even if he told me to. Anyway, he knows the mystery. He's told me about it.'

Mr Goon pricked up his ears at once. What! Fatty had got hold of another mystery! What could it be? Mr Goon could have danced with rage. That boy! A real pest he was, if ever there was one.

'Now, you look here!' he said to Ern, 'It's your duty to report to me anything that boy tells you about this mystery. See?'

Ern was torn between his urgent wish to be loyal to Fatty, the boy he admired so tremendously, and his fear that Mr Goon might punish him if he refused to tell anything Fatty told him.

'Go on,' said his uncle. 'Tell me what you know. It's your bound duty to tell a police officer everything. What's this here wonderful mystery?'

'Oh – it's just lights flashing on Christmas Hill,' stammered poor Ern. 'That's about all I know, Uncle. I don't believe Fatty knows much more. He's given me a notebook – look! You can see what's written down in it. Hardly anything.'

Mr Goon frowned over the headings. He began to plan. He could always get this notebook from Ern

– and if the boy refused to give it to him, well then, as an officer of the law he'd get it somehow – even if he had to do it when Ern was asleep. He gave it back to Ern.

'Well then, you see you report to me all the goings-on that those kids get up to,' said Mr Goon.

'Yes Uncle,' said Ern, not meaning to at all. He backed away from his uncle. 'There aren't any goings-on just now. We hadn't planned anything, Uncle. You came and interrupted us.'

'And a good thing too,' said Mr Goon. 'Now you can just sit down at the kitchen table and do some holiday work, see? Time you did something to oil those brains of yours. I'm not going to have you tearing about with those five kids and that dog all day long.'

Ern went obediently to the kitchen and settled down at the table with an arithmetic book. He had had a bad report from his school the term before, and was supposed to do quite a bit of holiday work. But instead of thinking of his sums, he thought about the Find-Outers, especially Fatty and the mystery, and flashing lights, and kidnappers and robbers. Lovaduck! How exciting it all was.

Ern was worried because his uncle wouldn't let him go out. He couldn't get in touch with the others if he didn't go out. Suppose they went to look for those flashing lights and didn't let him know? Ern felt he simply couldn't *bear* that.

All that day he was kept in the house. He went to bed to dream of tigers, crocodiles, Fatty reciting verse and somebody kidnapping his uncle. When he awoke the next morning, he began to plan how to get in touch with the others.

But Mr Goon had other plans. 'You can take down all those files on those shelves,' he said. 'And clean up the shelves and dust the files, and put them back in proper order.'

That took Ern all morning. Mr Goon went out and Ern hoped one of the Find-Outers would come, but they didn't. In the afternoon, Mr Goon settled himself down to go to sleep as usual. He saw Ern looking very down in the dumps and was pleased. 'He won't go snooping again!' he thought. 'He knows what he'll get if he does!'

And Mr Goon went peacefully off to sleep. He was awakened by a thunderous knocking at the door. He almost leapt out of his chair, and Ern looked alarmed.

'Shall I go, Uncle?' he said.

Mr Goon did not answer. He went to the door himself, buttoning up his uniform. That knocking sounded official. It might be the Inspector himself. People didn't usually hammer on the door of a police officer like that. They'd be afraid to!

Outside stood a fat old woman in a red shawl. 'I've come to complain,' she began, in a high, quavering voice. 'The things I've put up with from that woman! She's my next-door neighbour, sir, and she's the meanest woman you ever saw. She throws her rubbish into my garden, sir, and she always lights her bonfire when the wind's blowing my way, and . . .'

'Wait, wait,' said Mr Goon, annoyed. 'What's your name and where do . . .'

'And only yesterday she called me a monster, sir, that was the very word she used, oh, a wicked woman she is, and I won't stand for it any longer. Why, last week her dustbin . . .'

Mr Goon saw that this would go on forever. 'You can put in a written complaint,' he said. 'I'm busy this afternoon,' and he shut the door firmly.

He settled himself down in his chair again, but

before two minutes had gone, there came such a knock at the door that it was a wonder it wasn't broken down. Mr Goon, in a fury, leapt up again and almost ran to the door. The woman was there again, her arms folded akimbo over her chest.

'I forgot to tell you, sir,' she began, 'when I put my washing out last week this woman threw a pail of dirty water over it, and I had to wash it all again, and . . .'

'Didn't I tell you to put in a written report?' roared Mr Goon. 'Do as you're told!' And again he shut the door, and stamped into the kitchen, fuming.

No sooner had he sat down than the knocker sounded again. Mr Goon looked at Ern. 'You go,' he said. 'It's that woman again. Tell her what you like.'

Ern went, rather scared. He opened the door and a flood of words poured over him. 'Och, it's you this time, is it? Well, you tell your uncle, what's the good of me putting in a written report when I can't read nor write? You ask him that. You go in and ask him that!'

And then, to Ern's enormous astonishment, the red-shawled woman dug him in the chest, and said in a whisper, 'Ern! Take this! Now, tell me to go away, quick!'

Ern gaped. That was Fatty's voice, surely? Coo, was this Fatty in one of his disguises? Wonderful! Fatty winked hugely, and Ern found his voice.

'You clear orf!' he cried. 'Bothering my uncle like this! I won't have it! Clear orf, I say!'

He slammed the door. Mr Goon, in the kitchen, listened in astonishment. Why, Ern had been able to get rid of the woman far more quickly than he had. There must be something in the boy after all.

Ern was quickly reading the note Fatty had pushed into his hand.

> Tonight. Watch for lights on Christmas Hill.
> Hide in ditch by mill. Midnight. Report
> tomorrow.

Ern stuffed the note into his pocket, too thrilled for words. It was beginning! He was plunging into a mystery! And he wouldn't tell his uncle a single word. That Fatty! Fancy having the cheek to dress up like that and come thundering on his uncle's front door. Ern went into the kitchen, quite bemused.

'So you got rid of that woman?' said his uncle. 'Well, let's hope she won't come hammering again.'

She didn't. She went home to Fatty's house, slipped out of her things in Fatty's shed – and there was Fatty himself, taking off the woman's wig he wore, and rubbing away the wrinkles he had painted on his face. He chuckled. That took Mr Goon in properly! My word, Ern's face was a picture when he saw it was me!

7. MYSTERIOUS HAPPENINGS ON CHRISTMAS HILL

Ern was in such a state of excitement all the rest of the day that his uncle couldn't help noticing it. He stared at Ern and wondered. What was up with the boy? He hadn't seen or heard from the others. Then why was he so excited? He couldn't keep still for a minute.

'Stop fidgeting, Ern!' said Mr Goon sharply. 'What's the matter with you?'

'Nothing Uncle,' said Ern. Actually Ern was a bit worried about something. He knew Christmas Hill all right – but he didn't know where this mill was that Fatty had mentioned in his letter. How could he find out? Only by asking his uncle. But would his uncle smell a rat if he began talking about the mill?

He decided to get a map of the district out of the bookcase and study it. So when Mr Goon was answering the telephone, Ern slid the map from the shelf, opened it and looked for the mill. Oh yes

– there it was – on the right of the stream. If he followed the stream he couldn't help coming to the mill. Ern shivered in delight when he thought of creeping out all by himself that night. He marked where the mill was, and then with his pencil followed the way he would go, right up to the mill.

Mr Goon's eyes looked sharply at the map as he came back into the room. 'What you studying? he asked.

'Oh – just looking at a map of this district to see if I can go for a good walk somewhere,' said Ern. He put the map back, and felt the little note in his pocket. Nothing would make him show it to Mr Goon. Ah, that was a clever trick of Fatty's getting him a message through, right under Mr Goon's nose!

Mr Goon knew there was something up, especially when Ern said he would pop off to bed early. That wasn't like Ern! He watched him go, and then took out from the shelf the map that he had seen Ern using. He at once saw the pencilled path from the village of Peterswood to the old mill on Christmas Hill.

So that's where something's going on! said Mr Goon to himself. Lights flashing on Christmas Hill –

which means somebody's there that's got no business to be. And the person to look into this is PC Goon. There's no time like the present, either. I'll go tonight!

Quite a lot of people were preparing to go to Christmas Hill that night! Pip and Larry were going, complete with torches, and red, blue and green coloured paper to slip over the beam now and again. Fatty was going, of course, to give Ern a fright. Ern was going – and so was Mr Goon. A real crowd!

Mr Goon didn't go to bed that night. It wasn't worth it. He planned to slip off at about half past eleven, very quietly so as not to wake Ern.

Ern, as a matter of fact, was wide awake, listening to the church clock striking the half hours. He shivered with excitement in his warm bed. He didn't hear Mr Goon go quietly out of the front door and pull it to behind him. He was quite sure his uncle was in bed and asleep, as he usually was at that hour.

About two minutes after Mr Goon had gone from the house, Ern got up. He was fully dressed. He took his torch and tried it. Yes, it was all right. Bit faint, but it would last. He pulled on a coat, stuffed a scarf round his neck, and put on his big cap. He trod quietly down the stairs, hoping not to wake up his uncle – who by this time was plodding softly up Christmas Hill.

Fatty was already by the mill, hidden safely under a bush. Larry and Pip were some distance away, each with a torch and directions to begin shining them here and there, to and fro, every few minutes, in the direction of the mill. The hill was a desolate, deserted place, and the wind was very cold as it swept across it that night.

Mr Goon wished he was home safe and warm in bed. He plodded along quietly, thinking of comforting things like hot cocoa and hot water bottles. And quite suddenly he saw a light flashing not far from him!

Mr Goon sank down on the hillside beside a hedge. So that toad of a boy was right. There *was* something going on after all on Christmas Hill! What could it be?

He watched intently, almost forgetting to breathe. A red light – flash-flash! A green one – flash-flash-flash! And gracious, there was another light further up the hill – a blue one, flash!

Larry and Pip were enjoying themselves, flashing their torches, hoping that Ern was seeing the flashes and marvelling. Fatty was waiting impatiently for

68

Ern. Where was he? All this flashing was being wasted if Ern wasn't seeing it. Surely he hadn't gone to sleep in bed when he had been told to come to the mill?

Then Fatty heard a sigh as if someone was letting out a big breath. Ah – that must be Ern. He must be hiding somewhere nearby. Perhaps he didn't quite know where the mill was.

Flash-flash-flash! The lights winked out over the hill. Mr Goon wondered if they were being flashed in Morse code, but after trying hard to puzzle out any letters being flashed he gave up. Who were these signallers? Were they flashing to somebody in the old deserted mill? Mr Goon thought about the mill. It was almost ruined. He was positive there was nothing to be found there but rats and owls.

Mr Goon moved his cramped legs and a twig cracked sharply under him. He held his breath again! Would anyone hear that? He listened and heard nothing. The lights went on and on flashing merrily. Most extraordinary. Mr Goon debated whether or not to tell the Inspector about it. He decided not to. He'd better get to the bottom of things before that cheeky Frederick Trotteville did.

The lights stopped flashing. They had been going strong for twenty minutes, and now Larry and Pip were so cold that they decided to make their way home. They would meet Fatty again in the morning, and hear what had happened to him and Ern. They chuckled as they thought of Ern, discovering Fatty crouching in a ditch, and wondered what he would do. Run away, probably.

When the lights stopped flashing, Mr Goon moved very cautiously from the hedge. He went down into some kind of ditch and tried to get a safe footing. Fatty heard him scraping about and had no doubt at all that it was Ern, watching lights flashing with wonder and fear.

Well, if Ern wasn't going to discover *him*, he had better discover Ern! He would leap on him and give him the fright of his life! They would have a good old rough and tumble!

Fatty crept towards Mr Goon. He decided to make a few noises first. So he made a mewing noise like a cat. Mr Goon stopped, surprised. A cat? Out here on Christmas Hill, with not a building near! Poor thing!

'Puss, puss, puss!' he called. Then he heard an

unmistakable clucking. '*Cluck*-luck-luck-luck-luck! *Cluck*-luck-luck-luck-luck!'

A hen! Who could it belong to? Mr Goon frowned. It must have escaped from somewhere – but where? There was no farm for miles!

Fatty then mooed like a cow. He was a good mooer and could even startle cows. He startled Mr Goon extremely, much more than he had ever startled cows. Mr Goon almost jumped out of his skin. A cow now! Visions of Christmas Hill suddenly populated in the middle of night with cows, cats and hens came into Mr Goon's mind. He couldn't understand it. For one moment, he wondered if he could be dreaming.

But he was too cold to be dreaming. He scratched the side of his cheek and puzzled about the cow. He ought to take a cow away from this bitter cold hill. He felt for his torch, and shone it all around, trying to find the cow. Fatty, crouched under a nearby bush, giggled. He thought it was Ern trying to see the cow, the cat and the hen. He debated whether to grunt like a pig or to wail like a baby.

He wailed, and Mr Goon froze to his very marrow. He was petrified. What else was abroad on

71

this dark hill tonight? Whatever there was, he wasn't going to waste any more time looking for it. He turned to run, and another wail made him shake at the knees.

Fatty stood up when he heard the noise of somebody running away. He couldn't let Ern go like that! He must go after him and pounce on him – and then he'd let him go – and perhaps Ern would spin such a wonderful tale to Old Clear-Orf about mysteries up on Christmas Hill that it would bamboozle the policeman completely.

So Fatty padded after Mr Goon. The policeman was terrified to hear somebody after him. He caught his foot on a root and fell flat on his face. Fatty fell over him. He was thoroughly enjoying himself.

But Ern seemed curiously strong! Fatty found himself heaved off, and a strong arm bent him back. A familiar voice grated in his ear. 'Ho, you would, would you? You come-alonga me!'

Now it was Fatty's turn to get a shock. Gracious, it was *Mr Goon*, not Ern. Fatty freed himself as soon as he could and shot off down the hill, praying that Mr Goon would not be able to put on his torch quickly enough to spot him.

His head was spinning. That was *Mr Goon*! Why was *he* there? Where was Ern? He went cold when he thought of what Mr Goon would say if he found out that it was Fatty who had leapt on him like that.

Mr Goon fumbled for his torch, but it had been broken in the rough and tumble. He was no longer frightened. He felt victorious. He had frightened off that fellow who had attacked him, whoever it was.

He must have been a big chap, thought Mr Goon, a big hefty strong chap. And I heaved him off as easy as winking. Flung himself on me, he did, like a ton of bricks! And me down flat on my face, too. Not a bad night's work really.

He made his way cautiously down the hill. He heard no more curious noises. Nobody else attacked him. He puzzled over the night's happenings and tried to sort them out.

Flashing lights – all colours – in two different places. A cat, a hen, a cow and something that wailed in a horrible manner. And a great giant of a fellow who attacked me out of the dark. That's something to go on! Can't make head nor tail of it now, but I'll get to the bottom of it!

Fatty made his way home too. Larry and Pip were

already home and in bed, hugging rather lukewarm hot water bottles. They were longing to see Fatty in the morning and to know what had happened to Ern. Had he been frightened of the lights? What did he do when he found Fatty crouching in the ditch?

Where *was* Ern?

He was having a little adventure all on his own!

8. ERN HAS AN ADVENTURE TOO

Ern, most unfortunately, had followed the wrong stream, so that it did not, of course, lead him to the mill on Christmas Hill. It meandered through frosty fields, and didn't go anywhere near a hill at all. Ern was rather astonished that he had no climbing to do, but he clung to the stream, hoping that sooner or later it would take him uphill.

If he had cared to flash his torch on the water he would have seen that the stream was going exactly the same way as he was, and could on no account be expected to run uphill, but Ern didn't think about that. He just went on and on.

He felt that it must be past midnight, and still there was no sign of a mill, and no sign of Christmas Hill either. He couldn't imagine where he was. He stumbled on over the frosty bank beside the little stream, following its curves.

Soon it was about half past twelve. Ern paused

and considered things. He must be going the wrong way. The others wouldn't have waited for him. They would probably have gone home after watching for the lights.

'I'd better go back,' said Ern, shivering. 'It's too cold. I don't care what the others say, I'd better go back.'

And then Ern suddenly saw a light! He was not expecting one and was extremely astonished. It suddenly shone out from some distance away and then faded. Could it possibly be part of the mystery?

Then he heard a noise. He listened. It was a low purring noise, like a car. It came from the same direction as the light he had seen. He couldn't see the car at all, but it must have passed down some path or lane not very far from him, because the purring of the engine grew louder and then faded again as the car was driven further and further away.

Why didn't it have lights? wondered Ern. He stood there, waiting and listening and then decided to move on a little further down the stream. He went cautiously, not liking to put on his torch.

Then he heard footsteps – soft footsteps walking nearby, crunching quietly over the frosty ground.

Two pairs of footsteps – or was it three? No, two.

A voice spoke softly in the darkness. 'Goodnight, Holland. See you later.'

There was an answering mumble, and then no other noise except departing footsteps. It sounded as if the two men had gone different ways.

Ern shivered with excitement and cold. He wished the others were there. Why weren't they? This must be part of the mystery Fatty had talked about. Then Fatty should have been there to share it with him. Were those men kidnappers or robbers or what?

Ern turned back. He put up his coat collar and tightened his scarf, for now he was meeting the wind. He kept close to the stream and walked over the frosted grass as fast as he could. Ooooh! It was cold!

He came at last to the bridge he knew, that crossed the stream and led into a little lane. He went up the lane, turned into the village street and made his way quietly to his uncle's house. He had been wise enough to take the backdoor key with him. He stole round to the back, and let himself in.

Mr Goon was now in bed, fast asleep and snoring. He didn't even know that Ern was out! He had crept upstairs, undressed, and got into bed with hardly a sound, not wanting to let Ern know he had been out at midnight. He didn't want him to guess he had been up to Christmas Hill, probing the mystery!

It took Ern a long time to go to sleep. To begin with he was very cold, and the bed didn't seem to warm up. And then he was puzzled by what he had seen and heard. It wasn't much – but it didn't make sense somehow. He thought he couldn't be a very good detective. That boy Fatty would have guessed a whole lot of things if he had been with Ern that night. Ern was quite sure of that.

Neither Mr Goon nor Ern said a word to each other of their midnight escapades. Mr Goon had a bruise on his cheek where his face had struck a stone when he had fallen. Ern had a scratch across his forehead where a bramble had scraped him. They both looked tired out.

'You do what you like today, Ern,' said Mr Goon, who felt that Ern might probably pick up a few clues from Fatty about the mystery, and pass them on to him – or if he wrote them down in his notebook he could get them when Ern was asleep and read them.

'Thanks Uncle,' said Ern, perking up at once. Now

he would be able to go and see the others and hear what had happened.

He went round to Fatty's shed, but Fatty wasn't there. However, there was a message up on the door. 'Gone to Pip's. Join us there.'

Guessing correctly that the message was for him, Ern went up to Pip's. Bets saw him from the window and waved to him.

She opened the window. 'Don't go to the front door. Come in the garden door at the side of the house, and wipe your feet for goodness' sake!'

Ern did as he was told.

'Hello,' said Fatty, when he came in at the playroom door. 'You saw the message then. What happened to you last night? You went to sleep and didn't wake up in time to come, I suppose?'

'I didn't go to sleep at all!' said Ern indignantly. 'I got up and followed the stream – but it didn't lead me to Christmas Hill, or to any mill. I don't know where it led me to. But I saw the mysterious light all right.'

'You didn't,' said Larry. 'Pip and I and Fatty were up on the hill and saw them. You couldn't *possibly* have seen any flashing lights if you weren't up on the hill.'

'Well, I did then,' said Ern, looking annoyed. 'You weren't with me. You don't know *what* I saw!'

'Did you tell your uncle that we had told you to go to the mill on Christmas Hill last night?' demanded Fatty.

''Course I didn't,' said Ern, even more annoyed. 'He was in bed and snoring!'

'He wasn't,' said Fatty. 'He was up on Christmas Hill.'

Ern didn't believe him at all. 'Oh, goanborlyered!' he said in a disgusted voice.

The Find-Outers looked inquiringly at him. What did this peculiar word mean? 'What did you say then?' asked Fatty. 'Is it Spanish or something?'

'I said "Goanborlyered,"' repeated Ern. 'And fry your face too!'

The second part of what he said threw light on the first part. 'Oh! He said "Go and boil your head!,"' explained Daisy.

'SwatIsaid,' said Ern looking sulky.

'SwatIsaid,' said Fatty. 'What's the matter, Ern? Why don't you believe me when I say your uncle was up on the hill last night?'

'Because I heard him snoring like mad when I got in, that's all,' said Ern.

'Did you hear snoring like mad when you went out?' asked Fatty. Ern considered, frowning hard.

'No. Can't say I did. He *might* have gone out without me hearing him, and come back before I did.'

'That's what he did then,' said Fatty. 'But what I can't make out is – why did he go up? How did he know anything about meeting at the mill on Christmas Hill?'

'He might somehow have got hold of the note you gave Ern when you disguised yourself as the red-shawled woman,' said Daisy. 'He'd know then.'

'Yes. I suppose that's what he must have done – if Ern was silly enough to give him the chance,' said Fatty.

'Well, I didn't,' said Ern. 'What you all getting at me this morning for? I got up, didn't I, and I tried to get to Christmas Hill? I must have followed the wrong stream, that's all. I looked up the mill on the map and I saw that if I could follow the stream that runs down by it, I'd get there all right. But it was dark and I couldn't see anything. But I tell you I did see a light.' Everyone felt certain that Ern was making this up, just as they had made up their flashing lights! Ern went on, trying to impress the others that he really was telling the truth.

'I was standing by the stream, see. And I saw this light. It just shone out once and then faded. Then I heard a purring noise and a car came by somewhere – and it hadn't any lights on. That was strange, and I thought maybe it was all part of the mystery too.'

The others were listening now. Ern went on, warming up a little. 'Well then, after the car had gone, I heard footsteps – two pairs – and then I heard one man say to the other, "Goodnight, Holland. See you later", or something like that. And after that I turned back and went home.'

There was silence. Everyone believed Ern now. If he had been making his tale up he would have pretended that he had seen many lights, heard more than one car, and more than two men. Because it was a simple story, it seemed as if it might be true.

'Have you told your uncle this?' asked Fatty at last.

'No,' said Ern. There was a pause. Then Ern remembered something. 'I put that notebook back,' he said, 'and Uncle found me just shutting the drawer. He said I was snooping round to find out things for you. I'm not telling my uncle a thing now!'

'You shouldn't have taken the notebook in the

first place,' said Fatty. 'Then you wouldn't have had to put it back and you wouldn't have been discovered.'

Ern scowled, partly because he knew Fatty was right and partly because he didn't like having it said to him in such a candid manner. But Fatty always said what he thought, and nothing would stop him.

'Look here,' said Ern suddenly, 'which mystery is the real one? The one you mean, with flashing lights on Christmas Hill – or mine, down by the stream? Or are they both real?'

Fatty rubbed his nose. He didn't quite know what to say. His had been made up, but he didn't want to admit that. Neither did he want Ern to think there might be any mystery in what *he* had seen and heard the night before, in case there really *was*. If there was, Fatty didn't want Ern blundering into it and telling his uncle everything.

'I suppose,' said Ern, answering his own question, 'the mystery up on the hill's the real one – or else uncle wouldn't have gone up there, would he?'

'He must have thought there was something going on there,' agreed Fatty.

'And there was,' said Pip, with a little giggle.

'Well, Ern, what about you going up on Christmas Hill to see if you can find a few clues in daylight,' said Fatty. 'They would be a help.'

'What sort of clues?' asked Ern, looking cheerful again.

'Oh – cigarette-ends, buttons, footprints, anything like that,' said Fatty. 'You just never know. A real detective can usually find no end of clues.'

'I'll go up about three,' said Ern. 'Uncle will be having his afternoon snooze then. Well – I'd better be going. I'll bring any clues to you if I find them. So long!'

9. LOTS OF CLUES FOR ERN!

The Find-Outers looked at each other when Ern had disappeared. 'What do you think, Fatty?' said Larry. 'Anything in what he said?'

'I don't know,' said Fatty slowly. 'It seems a bit odd, doesn't it? – a light in the middle of the night – a car suddenly appearing without lights – and then voices. What did he say the one man said to the other?'

' "Goodnight, Holland. See you later," ' said Larry.

'Yes, that's it. Wonder how Ern managed to remember the name Holland, and if he heard it right,' said Fatty.

'Any use having a snoop along the stream to see if we can spy anything?' asked Larry.

'Not allowed to,' said Pip at once.

'Well – it's not a mystery *yet*, and may never *be*,' said Larry. 'So I don't see why we shouldn't at least go for a walk along the stream.'

'With Ern?' asked Bets.

'I don't know,' said Fatty. 'He'll probably go and tell everything to Mr Goon. Still, Mr Goon has got plenty to think of at the moment. He's seen masses of lights on Christmas Hill, heard a cow, a hen, a cat and a baby up there, and struggled with an unknown attacker. Quite a nice little mystery for him to be getting on with!'

The others laughed. They had roared at Fatty's account of what had happened the night before, and his amazement at finding the person by the hedge was Mr Goon, not Ern.

'I think one of the best things we can do is to go up to Christmas Hill before three o'clock, and drop a nice meaty lot of clues,' said Fatty. 'Ern will find them and glory in them – probably write some portry about them. And if he hands them over to Mr Goon, so much the better!'

So, in great glee, the Five Find-Outers and Buster set off up Christmas Hill, taking with them what they thought would do for clues. It was a fine sunny day, but cold, and they got nice and warm going up the hill. Their parents were pleased to see them going out. Nobody liked all the five indoors. Some noisy game always seemed to develop sooner or later.

'Here's where I fought Mr Goon last night,' said Fatty, showing where he and Mr Goon had rolled in the ditch. 'I got an awful shock when I found it was Mr Goon. He's strong, you know. He almost caught me. What a row I'd have got in if he'd seen it was me!'

'Let's put a clue here,' said Larry. 'A torn-off button with a bit of cloth attached. Very good clue!'

'Where did you get it?' said Daisy. 'You'll get into trouble if you tore it off one of your coats.'

'Idiot! I tore it off the old coat that's hung in the garage for ages,' said Larry, and threw the brown button down, with its bit of brown cloth attached to it. 'Clue number one.'

'Here's clue number two,' said Pip, and put down a bit of paper, on which he had scribbled a telephone number. 'Peterswood 0160.'

'Whose number's that?' asked Fatty at once.

'Oh, nobody's,' said Pip. 'I just made it up.'

'Your fingerprints will be on it,' said Fatty, who always thought of things like that.

'No they won't,' said Pip. 'I tore it out of a new notebook, with gloves on my hands, and I've carried it in my gloved hands all the way. So there!'

'You're getting quite clever,' said Fatty, pleased. 'Right. That's clue number two. Here's clue number three.'

He threw down a cigar-stump that he had found in the gutter.

'That's a good clue,' said Larry. 'Robber smokes Corona cigars. Mr Goon will love that if he gets it from Ern.'

'I've got a clue too,' said Bets. 'A red shoelace, broken in half and dirtied!'

'Yes. Very good, Bets,' said Fatty, approvingly. 'I like the way you've dirtied it. Ern will be thrilled to pick that up.'

They went on a little way further, nearer the mill. Daisy still had her clue to dispose of. It was a very old ragged handkerchief with a K embroidered in one corner.

'K,' said Fatty. I can't think of anyone we know beginning with K. Whose was it?'

'Don't know,' said Daisy with a laugh. 'I picked it up by the hedge that runs by Pip's garden!'

'I hope the wind won't blow any of our clues away,' said Larry anxiously.

'I don't expect so,' said Fatty. 'It's a calm day.

Come on, let's get back before we meet Ern coming up here.'

They ran down the hill. At the bottom, they met Mr Goon labouring along on his bicycle, very angry because his snooze had been interrupted by a call about a stolen dog. When he saw the children at the bottom of Christmas Hill, he stopped in suspicion.

'What you been doing up there?' he asked.

'Having a lovely walk, Mr Goon,' said Fatty, in the polite voice that always sent Mr Goon into a frenzy. Buster, who had been left some way behind with his nose in a rabbit-hole, now came rushing up in delight.

'You keep him off,' said Mr Goon, fixing them all with a protruding eye. 'And if I was you – I'd keep away from Christmas Hill.'

'Oh, Mr Goon, but why?' asked Fatty, in such an innocent voice that Mr Goon began to go purple. That cheeky toad!

'It's such a nice hill to run down,' said Pip.

'Now, don't *you* start!' said Mr Goon, slowly swelling up in rage. 'And take my advice – don't you go up Christmas Hill again!'

'Can we come down it?' asked Larry and the

others went off into shouts of laughter to see Mr Goon trying to work this out.

'Any more cheek from you,' he began, 'and . . .'

At this moment Buster, who had been struggling for all he was worth in Fatty's arms, leapt right out of them almost on top of Mr Goon. The policeman hurriedly got on his bicycle. 'You clear orf!' he shouted to Buster and the children too. He rode up the lane at top speed, trying to shake the dog off, and almost collided with Ern, who was on his way to search for clues up Christmas Hill.

'Out of my way!' yelled Mr Goon, nearly running over Ern's toes. Buster ran between Ern's legs and he fell over at once. In joy and delight, Buster stopped to sniff round this fresh person, and found it was Ern. He leapt on him and began to lick him, while Mr Goon pedalled thankfully up the road, getting redder and redder as he went.

'Your uncle's in a bit of a rage,' said Fatty. 'It's not good for him to ride a bike at such speed. You ought to warn him. It must be bad for his heart.'

'It would be, if he had one,' said Ern. 'Well, I'm going to do what you said – hunt for clues. You coming too?'

'No, we've got to get home,' said Fatty. 'I hope you find a few, Ern. Let us know if you do. That's the sign of a good detective, you know, to be able to spot clues.'

Ern glowed. If there were any clues to be found on the hill, he'd find them! He badly wanted Fatty to admire him. He took out his notebook and opened it.

'I wrote a pome about last night,' he said. 'It's called *The Dark, Dark Night*.'

'Fine!' said Fatty hastily. 'Pity we can't wait and hear it. Don't be too long before you go up the hill, Ern, or you'll find yourself in the dark, dark night up there again. Follow the stream and you'll come to the mill.'

They parted, and Ern put his notebook away. He took out his other notebook, the one Fatty had given him. He opened it at the page marked CLUES. How he hoped to be able to make a list there before the afternoon was done.

The others went home. Fatty was rather silent. Bets walked close beside him, not interrupting his thoughts. She knew he was trying to puzzle something out.

'Pip, have you got a good map of the district?' said

Fatty, as they came to Pip's house. 'If you have I'll just come in and have a squint at it. Somebody's borrowed ours.'

'Yes. Dad keeps one on the shelf,' said Pip. 'But for goodness sake, put it back when you've finished with it.'

'Course I will,' said Fatty, and they went in. Pip found the map and they took it upstairs. Fatty put his finger on Peterswood, their village. He traced the way up to the mill, up the stream on Christmas Hill. Then he traced another way, alongside another stream, that at first ran near the first one and then went across the fields.

'I think this must be the stream Ern went by last night,' he said. 'Let's see where it flows past. Nothing much, look! Just fields.'

The others all bent over the map, breathing down Fatty's neck. They watched his finger go along the stream. It came to where a thick wood was marked. In the middle of the wood some kind of building was shown.

'Now I wonder what building that is,' said Fatty, thoughtfully. 'Anyone been along that way?'

Nobody had. Nobody even knew the wood very

well, though they had sometimes passed it. Not one of them had known there was any building in the wood.

'We'll ask about it,' said Fatty, getting up. 'Gosh, I must go. I'm supposed to be going out for tea with Mummy. Awful thought. You know, I do believe there may be something in Ern's story. Cars that leave a wood in the middle of the night without lights need a bit of looking into.'

The others looked excited. 'Is it a mystery, Fatty?' asked Bets eagerly. 'Do say it is! Wouldn't it be funny if we did tumble into the middle of a real mystery just because we invented one for Ern.'

'It would,' said Fatty. 'Well, we shall see. Won't Ern be thrilled when he finds all those clues? He'll come rushing along tomorrow!'

'I hope I won't giggle,' said Bets.

'You dare!' said Pip. 'Good-bye, Fatty. Behave yourself at tea, and be a dear, well-mannered child!'

'Oh, goanborlyered!' said Fatty rudely, and off he went, with shouts of laughter following him.

10. MR GOON AND ERN

Ern had a simply wonderful time up on Christmas Hill, collecting clues. It was a lovely afternoon and he walked slowly up the hill, his eyes on the ground. He felt important. The beginnings of a 'pome' swam into his mind, as he looked up and saw the sun sinking redly in the west.

Pore dying sun that sinks to rest, thought Ern, and felt excited and pleased. That was a good line, a very good one indeed. Ern never wrote a cheerful 'pome'. They were all very, very sad, and they made Ern feel deliciously sad too.

He walked on, his eyes on the ground, thinking about the dying sun. He suddenly saw a piece of rag fluttering and picked it up. Nobody could tell what colour it had been. Ern looked at it. Was it a clue? He pondered over it. He wished he was like Fatty, able to tell at a glance what things were clues and what weren't.

He put it into his overcoat pocket. Fatty would know. He cast his eyes on the ground again. Aha! What was this in the ditch? A button! Yes, with a bit of brown cloth attached to it. Surely that was a clue? Ern looked at the ground in the ditch, and noted the broken twigs and the way the frosty ground was rubbed and scraped. Been somebody here! thought Ern in excitement. And this button's off his coat. That's a big clue, a really meaty one.

He put that in his pocket too. He was feeling really thrilled now. Two clues already!

He found the broken shoelace. He found the cigar-end and sniffed at it in a very knowing manner. 'Ha! A good cigar! Whoever was here has money to spend. I'm getting on. I see a man with a brown coat with brown buttons, smoking a good cigar, and wearing reddish laces in his shoes. I don't know about that bit of rag. That doesn't fit in somehow.'

He picked up an empty cigarette packet. It had held 'Players' cigarettes. 'Coo! He smokes cigarettes as well!' said Ern, feeling cleverer and cleverer. That went into his pocket too. He was getting on! Who would have thought there were so many clues left carelessly lying about like that? No wonder detectives went hunting for them after a robbery.

He picked up a broken tin next. It looked as if it had possibly been a tin of boot polish, but it was so old and rusty that there was no telling what it might have been. Anyway it went into his pocket too.

Then he found Pip's bit of paper blowing about. Ern picked it up. Lovaduck! Now we're getting hot! This is somebody's telephone number – in Peterswood too. I'm really getting hot! Pity Fatty didn't come up with me – we'd have had a fine time collecting clues!

He then found Daisy's ragged old handkerchief, embroidered with a K in the corner. This seemed a first class clue. K! he thought. K for Kenneth. K for Katie. Or it might be a surname of course. Can't tell. That went into his pocket as well.

After that, he only found two more things that seemed worth picking up. One was a burnt match, the other was the stub of a pencil. It had initials cut into it at the end. E.H.

With a pocketful of interesting clues, Ern went down the hill again. It was getting dark. He would have liked to stay longer and find more clues but he couldn't see clearly any longer. Anyway he had done well, he felt.

When he got home, his uncle was out. Ern got himself some tea, then took out his notebook and opened it at the page marked CLUES.

He sharpened his pencil and set to work to put down a list of all the things he had found.

CLUES

1. *Piece of rag*
2. *Brown button with bit of cloth*
3. *Broken shoelace, reddish colour*
4. *End of good cigar*
5. *Empty cigarette packet ('Players')*
6. *Broken tin, very rusty*
7. *Bit of paper with telephone number*
8. *Ragged handkerchief, K in corner*
9. *Burnt match*
10. *Pencil, very short, E.H. on it.*

'Look at that', said Ern in satisfaction. 'Ten clues already! Not a bad bit of work. I'd make a good detective. Lovaduck! Here's uncle!'

Mr Goon could be heard coming into the little

hall, and a familiar cough sounded. In haste, Ern swept all the clues into his pocket, and was just stuffing his notebook away when his uncle came in. Ern looked so guilty that Mr Goon was suspicious at once. Now what had that boy been up to?

'Hello Uncle,' said Ern.

'What you doing sitting at an empty table, doing nothing?' said Mr Goon.

'I'm not doing anything,' said Ern. Mr Goon gave a snort.

'I can see that. What you been doing this afternoon?'

'I've been for a walk,' said Ern.

'Where?' said Mr Goon. 'With those five kids?'

'No. By myself,' said Ern. 'It was such a nice afternoon.'

Ern was not in the habit of taking walks by himself, and Mr Goon looked at him suspiciously again. What *was* the boy up to? How much did he know?

'Where did you go?' he asked again.

'Up Christmas Hill,' said Ern. 'It – it was awfully nice up there. The view, you know, Uncle.'

Mr Goon sat down ponderously in his armchair and gazed solemly at Ern. 'Now, you look here, my boy,' he said, 'you're up to something with those pestering kids. Oh yes, you are, so don't try to say you aren't. Now, you and me, we must work together. We're uncle and nephew, aren't we? In the interests of the law, we must tell each other all the goings-on.'

'What goings-on?' asked Ern in alarm, wondering how much his uncle knew. He was beginning to feel frightened. He put his hand into his pocket to feel the clues there. He mustn't tell his uncle about them. He must keep them all for Fatty and the others.

'You know quite well what the goings-on are,' said Mr Goon, beginning to remove his boots. 'Up Christmas Hill! Didn't you tell me about the lights flashing there?'

'Yes,' said Ern. 'But that's all I told you, Uncle. What other goings-on do you mean?'‑

Mr Goon began to lose his temper. He stood up in his stockinged feet and advanced on poor Ern, who hadn't even a chance of getting up from his chair and backing away.

'I'm going to lose my temper with you, Ern,' said Mr Goon. 'I can feel it. You be a good boy, and work with me, and everything will be fine. See? Now you tell me what that boy, Frederick, told you.'

Ern gave in. He hadn't any courage at all. He knew he was a poor weak thing, but he couldn't seem to help it.

'He said there were two gangs,' blubbered Ern. 'Kidnappers was one gang. Robbers was the other.'

Mr Goon stared at Ern in surprise. This was news! 'Go on!' he said disbelievingly. 'Kidnappers and robbers! What next!'

'And lights flashing on Christmas Hill,' went on Ern. 'Well, I don't know about that, Uncle. I haven't seen any lights there at all.'

Mr Goon had though! He looked thoughtfully at Ern. That bit of the tale was true anyway – about the lights flashing, because he had seen them himself the night before – so the other part might be true too. Kidnappers and robbers! Now *how* did that boy Frederick get to know these things? He brooded about Fatty for a little while and thought of quite a lot of things he would like to do to him.

It was very, very necessary to make sure that Ern told him everything in future. Mr Goon could see that. He decided it would be best not to frighten Ern any more. He must win his friendship! That was the line to follow.

So, to Ern's enormous surprise, Mr Goon suddenly patted him on the shoulder. Ern looked up in surprise and suspicion. Now what was Uncle up to?

'You were right to tell me, Ern, all that you've heard from those kids,' said Mr Goon in a kindly voice. 'Now you and me can work together, and we'll soon clean up this mystery – and we'll get no end of praise from Inspector Jenks. You've met him, haven't you? He said he thought you were a fine boy, and might help me no end.'

This wasn't true at all. Inspector Jenks had hardly glanced at Ern and, if he had, he certainly wouldn't have said such nice things about him. Poor Ern didn't shine in public at all, but looked very awkward and stupid.

Ern was relieved to see that his uncle was going to be friendly after all. All the same, Ern was very much ashamed of giving away all that Fatty had told him. Now his uncle would solve the mystery himself, arrest all the men, and Fatty and the other Find-Outers wouldn't have any fun.

'Anything else you can tell me, Ern?' said Mr Goon, putting on his enormous slippers.

'No, Uncle,' said Ern, wishing he hadn't got a pocketful of clues.

'What did you go up Christmas Hill this afternoon for?' asked Mr Goon.

'I told you. For a nice walk,' said Ern, looking sulky again. When would his uncle stop all this?

Mr Goon debated whether to go on cross-examining Ern or not. Perhaps not. He didn't want to make the boy obstinate. When he was safely asleep in bed that night he would get Ern's notebook out of his pocket and see if he had written anything down in it. Mr Goon picked up the paper and settled down for a read. Ern heaved a sigh of relief, and wondered if he could slip out to see the others. It was about six o'clock now – but Ern felt that he simply *must* tell Fatty all about the clues.

'Can I go out for a bit, Uncle?' he asked timidly. 'Just to slip round and have a talk with the others? They might have a bit of news for me.'

'All right,' said Mr Goon, turning a friendly face to Ern. 'You go. And get all you can out of them and then tell me the latest news. See?'

Ern lost no time. He pulled on his coat, took his scarf and fled out of the house. He made his way to

Pip's, because he remembered that Fatty was going out to tea that day.

He was lucky enough to find all the Find-Outers gathered together in Pip's playroom, under strict instructions from Mrs Hilton to take off their shoes if they wanted to play any games that meant running across the room. Fatty had just arrived, having dropped in on his way home with his mother, who was seeing Mrs Hilton for a few minutes downstairs.

'Guess what!' said Ern, bursting in suddenly. 'I've got ten clues for you! What do you think of that for a good day's work? I've got them all here!'

'Lovaduck!' said Fatty. 'Smazing! Smpossible! Swunderful! Let's have a look, Ern, quick!'

11. ERN'S CLUES

Ern pulled everything out of his pocket. When Bets saw all the things there that the Find-Outers had so carefully put on Christmas Hill for Ern to find, she wanted to giggle. But she saw Fatty's eye on her, and she didn't.

'See?' said Ern proudly. 'Cigar-end. That means somebody with money. And look here – he smokes cigarettes too – see this empty packet? And look – we want to look for somebody with a brown coat. And . . .'

'This is a very remarkable collection of clues, Ern,' said Fatty solemnly. 'I can see that Mr Goon's brains have been passed on to you. You take after him! A very remarkable afternoon's work.'

Ern was thrilled. Praise from Fatty was praise indeed. He showed every clue he had.

'Course, some of them mightn't be clues at all,' he admitted handsomely. 'I see that.'

'You're right,' said Fatty. 'You think of everything, Ern. This is all most interesting. It will help us tremendously.'

'Will it really?' said Ern delighted. Then his face clouded over. 'I've got something awful to tell you,' he said.

'What?' asked everyone, curiously.

'I went and gave the game away to my uncle,' said Ern dismally. He threatened me, so I went and told him about the kidnappers and the robbers up on Christmas Hill. You needn't call me a coward. I know that all right.'

He looked so completely miserable that the Five Find-Outers wanted to comfort him. Even Buster felt the same and put his front paws up on Ern's knee. Ern looked down at him gratefully.

'Well,' said Fatty, 'certainly it wasn't a brave thing to do, Ern, to give away somebody else's secret – but Mr Goon must have been very frightening. We won't tick you off.'

'He told me I must work with him,' said Ern, brightening up a little, as he saw the Find-Outers did not mean to cast him off. 'He said we were uncle and nephew, and we ought to work together.

I've got to tell him anything that happens.'

Fatty considered this. It suited him very well to have Mr Goon told all the things that didn't matter. It would serve him right for threatening poor Ern. Fatty did not like the streak of rage in Mr Goon.

'Well, there's something in that,' said Fatty. 'Yes, quite decidedly there's something in that. Families ought to work together. We shan't complain any more if you pass on any news to your uncle, Ern.'

'But I don't want to!' protested Ern at once. 'I want *you* to solve things, not Uncle. I don't want to work with Uncle.'

'Poor Ern!' Bets suddenly said. She could see very clearly how Ern was torn in two – he dearly wanted to work with the Find-Outers and be loyal to them – and he was terribly afraid he would have to help his uncle instead, because he was so frightened of him. All Ern needed was a little courage, but he hadn't got it.

'You'd better show these clues to your uncle,' said Fatty. 'Hadn't he, Larry? If they are going to work together, Mr Goon had better know about these. He'll think that Ern has done a fine piece of work.'

'I don't want to show him the clues,' said Ern

desperately. 'I tell you, I found them for you, not for Uncle.'

'Well, do what you like,' said Fatty. 'We shan't mind whether you show them or not. I suppose you wrote them all down in your notebook?'

'Oh yes,' said Ern proudly, and showed his long list. Fatty nodded approvingly.

'You didn't tell your uncle about how you went out alone last night, did you?' he said. It was very important that Mr Goon shouldn't know that. Ern shook his head.

'No. Course I didn't. I'm not telling him things he can't possibly guess. He'd be very angry if he knew I'd slipped out like that.'

'Tell us again about your little adventure,' said Fatty. So Ern obligingly told it. He used almost the same words as before, and all the Find-Outers felt that he was telling the exact truth.

'Are you certain that one man addressed the other as "Holland"?' asked Fatty.

'Oh yes. You see we did Holland in geography last term,' said Ern. 'So I knew the name all right.'

Well, that certainly seemed to fix the name. That might be very useful, thought Fatty. He got up to go, hearing his mother calling him from downstairs. Larry and Daisy got up too.

'There's Mummy ready to go,' said Fatty. 'Come on, Ern – you'd better go too.'

'I thought of a fine pome this afternoon,' said Ern, getting up. '*About the Dying Sun.*'

'We haven't time to hear it now,' said Daisy.

'Spitty,' said Fatty. Everyone but Ern knew what this meant. Ern looked at him in surprise.

'Spitty?' he said. 'What do you mean?'

'You heard me,' said Fatty. 'SPITTY!'

Bets went off into giggles. There came another call from downstairs. Fatty hurried to the door.

'He meant "It's a pity,"' giggled Bets.

'SwatIsaid,' said Fatty and disappeared with Larry and Daisy.

Ern, still rather bemused over the curious word Fatty had suddenly used, followed the three downstairs. He slipped out of the garden door unseen. He didn't want to meet Mrs Hilton, Pip's mother. He tore home to his uncle's house, hoping there was something nice for supper.

A delicious smell of bacon and eggs met him as soon as he got in. Ern stood and sniffed. Lovaduck!

Uncle was doing himself proud tonight. Ern wondered if he was going to get any bacon and eggs, or whether he would have to eat bread and cheese.

'Hurry up, young Ern!' called Mr Goon, in a jovial sort of voice that Ern had never heard before. 'I've fried you an egg and a bit of bacon. Hurry up!'

Ern hurried up. There was not only bacon and eggs but a bowl of tinned peaches and creamy custard. Ern took his place hungrily.

'Well? Did you see those kids? Get any news from them?' inquired Mr Goon affably, piling egg, bacon and toast onto Ern's plate.

'No. There wasn't any news, Uncle,' said Ern.

'But you must have talked about something,' said Mr Goon. 'What did they say to you?'

Ern racked his brains to think of something harmless to tell his uncle. He suddenly remembered something.

'I told them you said we were to work together,' he said.

'You shouldn't have told them that,' said Mr Goon, crossly. 'Now they won't tell you a thing!'

'Oh yes they will. They said it was right that an uncle and nephew should work together,' said Ern, shovelling egg and bacon into his mouth. 'And what's more, Fatty said I took after *you*, Uncle. He said you'd passed your brains on to *me*.'

Mr Goon looked most disbelievingly at Ern. He felt certain that Fatty didn't think much of any brains he possessed, and if he did he certainly wouldn't say so. He was just pulling Ern's leg. Mr Goon wished in exasperation that Ern wasn't so simple.

'He didn't mean that, see?' said Mr Goon. 'He can't think much of *your* brains, Ern. You know you haven't got any to speak of. You think of your last school report.'

Ern thought instead of the remarkable set of clues he had found that afternoon. He smiled. 'Oh, I've got brains all right, Uncle. You wait and see.'

Mr Goon felt that he was about to lose his temper again. He just simply couldn't be more than ten minutes with Ern without feeling annoyed and aggravated. His ears turned red, and Ern saw them and felt uncomfortable. He knew that was a danger sign. What *could* he have said now to annoy his uncle?

He ate his peaches and custard in silence, and so did Mr Goon. Then, still in silence, Ern did the washing-up and, after that, got out his books to do some work. Mr Goon, trying to look pleased so as not to make Ern obstinate, sat reading his paper again. He looked up approvingly as Ern sat down to work.

'That's right, my boy. That's the way to get brains like mine. A bit of hard study will make a lot of difference to you.'

'Yes, Uncle,' said Ern, resting his head on his hands as if he was learning something. But Ern was going over his clues, one by one. He was thinking of robbers and kidnappers. He was up on Christmas Hill, waiting for desperate men to do desperate deeds. Oh, Ern was far, far away from his geography book on the kitchen table!

He went to bed early because he was tired. He fell asleep at once, and did little snores like Mr Goon's big ones. Mr Goon heard them from downstairs and rose quietly. Now to get Ern's notebook and see what he had written in it! If Ern wouldn't tell him everything, Mr Goon meant to find it out. No harrassing thoughts of being mean or deceitful entered Mr Goon's mind. He thought himself duty-bound to sneak Ern's notebook from his pocket!

Ern did not stir when Mr Goon tiptoed in. His uncle slipped his hand into the coat pocket and found the notebook at once. He felt the trousers and decided to take them downstairs and see what was crowding the pockets.

He sat down at the table to study Ern's notebook. It fell open at the page headed CLUES. Mr Goon's eyes grew round as they saw the long, long list.

'Look at that! All them clues and never a word to me about them. The young limb! I'd like to skin him!'

He read down the list. Then an idea occurred to him and he put his hand into Ern's trouser pocket. Out came the ten clues, tumbling on the table. Mr Goon took a deep breath and stared at them.

A button and a bit of cloth! Now that was a very, very important clue. And this cigar-end. Expensive! Mr Goon sniffed it. He picked up the clues one by one and considered them carefully. Which of them would have any real bearing on the happenings up on Christmas Hill?

Should he tell Ern he had found the clues or not? No, better not. Ern might tell Fatty and the others, and they would have plenty to say about Mr Goon's methods of getting hold of things. Mr Goon took a little snipping of the cloth attached to the button so that he would have a piece to match up with the coat, should he be fortunate enough to meet anyone wearing it. He took a note of the Peterswood number. Whose was it?

He rang directory enquiries to find out. The number belonged to a Mr Lazarinsky. Ha – that sounded most suspicious. Mr Goon made a mental note to keep an eye on Mr Lazarinsky. So far as he knew, the man was a harmless old fellow who spent most of his time growing roses and chrysan-themums. But you never know. That might be a cover for all kinds of dirty work.

Mr Goon replaced everything in Ern's pockets, the notebook as well. Ern didn't stir when he tiptoed out of the bedroom. Mr Goon felt that he had done a good evening's work. He wondered how much Fatty knew about this curious mystery. It was funny that the Inspector hadn't sent him word of any possible goings-on in Peterswood.

Well, it would be a real pleasure to Mr Goon to open the Inspector's eyes, and show him that dirty work could go on under his very nose, in his own district – without people guessing anything. But he, Mr Goon, knew! He'd soon clear everything up – and perhaps this time he really *would* get promotion.

But even Mr Goon couldn't help feeling that this was rather doubtful!

12. A LITTLE INVESTIGATION

Fatty had been making a few inquiries. What was that building in the middle of the little wood? He asked his mother, who had never even heard of it. He asked the postman, who said it wasn't on his round, but he thought it was a ramshackle old place that had been used in the last war.

He found a directory of Peterswood, but it did not mention the building – only the wood, which it called Bourne Wood. The little stream that flowed through Peterswood was called the Bourne, so Fatty imagined the wood was named after it.

He didn't seem to be getting very far. He decided that it would be a very good idea to walk out to the wood and have a look round. So, the next morning, he went round to Larry and Daisy, collected them, and then went to fetch Pip and Bets. Buster came, of course, full of delight to think there was a walk for him.

'I thought we'd follow the stream, just like Ern did,' said Fatty. 'Then, when we come to about where he thought he was, we'll have a look round to see where that light he saw could have come from.'

The others were thrilled. 'Now mind!' said Fatty, '*you* are only going for a walk. Nothing to do with any mystery, so keep your minds easy. I'm the one that is mystery hunting!'

They all laughed. 'Right,' said Pip. 'But if we do happen to spot anything, we'll tell you, Fatty!'

Ern had not appeared so far, so they all set off without him. Fatty thought it was best anyhow. They didn't want to let Ern think there was any real mystery in what he had seen the other night, in case he said anything to Mr Goon. Let Mr Goon concentrate on Christmas Hill and the imaginary kidnappers and robbers!

They crossed the little bridge, and went along the bank beside the stream. It was still frosty weather and the grass crunched beneath their feet. The little stream wound in and out, and bare willow and alder trees grew here and there on its banks. The scene was a maze of wintry fields, dreary and desolate.

The stream wound endlessly through the fields.

Here and there, Fatty pointed to where Ern must have stumbled the other night, for marks were clearly to be seen on the frosty bank.

After some time, Bets pointed to the left. 'Look! Is that the wood over there?'

'Can't be,' said Pip. 'It's on our left instead of straight ahead.'

'I expect the stream winds to the left then,' said Fatty. And so it did. It suddenly took a left-hand bend and ran towards the dark wood.

The wood was made up of evergreen trees, and stood dark and still in the wintry air. Because the fir and pine trees still kept their foliage, dark green and thick, the wood somehow looked rather sinister.

'The trees are crouched together as if they are hiding something!' suddenly said Bets. Everyone laughed.

'Silly!' said Pip. But all the same they knew what Bets meant. They stood by the stream and looked at the wood. It did not seem very little now that they were near it. It seemed large and forbidding.

'I don't like it,' said Daisy. 'Let's go back.'

But she didn't mean that, of course. Nobody would have gone back just as they had got there.

They were all filled with curiosity to know what was so well hidden in those trees!

They followed the stream again until they had almost reached the wood. Not far off was a narrow lane, almost a cart-track, it was so rough.

Fatty stopped. 'Now,' he said, 'we know that a car went by not far from Ern, when he stood by the stream. It seems to me that the car must have gone down that lane. It must lead to the road that goes to Peterswood. I saw it on the map.'

'Yes,' said Larry. 'And this little lane or track must come from the middle of the wood – from whatever building is there. Let's go to the track and follow it.'

'Good idea,' said Fatty. 'Hey, Buster, come along. There can't be any rabbits down that hole – it's far too small!'

Buster left the rat-hole he was scraping at and ran to join them. They all jumped across the little stream, Buster too, and went towards the narrow track. They squeezed through the hedge and found themselves in a very small lane indeed, hardly wide enough to take a full-sized car!

'There are car tracks each side of the lane,' said Fatty, and the others saw tyre marks – many of them, all running almost on top of one another because the lane was so narrow. Two cars could not possibly pass.

'Come on – we'll go up the lane,' said Fatty. Then he lowered his voice. 'Now, not a word about anything except ordinary things. And if we're stopped, be surprised, scared and innocent. Don't say anything we don't want people to hear – we don't know when we may be overheard.'

A familiar thrill went through the Find-Outers as they heard Fatty's words. The mystery was beginning. They were perhaps walking into it. They had been forbidden to – but how could they tell, until they had walked into one, that a mystery was really and truly there?

The track wound about almost as much as the stream had done. Buster ran ahead, his tail wagging. He turned a corner ahead and then the children heard him barking.

They ran to see why. All they saw was a big pair of iron gates set into two enormous stone posts. A bell hung at one side. On each side of the posts stretched high walls, set with glass spikes at the top.

'Gracious! Is this the building?' said Bets in a whisper. Larry frowned at her, and she remembered she mustn't say anything unless it was quite ordinary. So she began to talk loudly about a game she had had for Christmas. The others joined in. They came near to the gates and then saw that a small lodge was on the other side.

They went to the great gates and pressed their faces to the wrought-iron work. Beyond the gates lay a drive, much better kept than the lane outside. Tall, dark trees lined the drive, which swept out of sight round a bend. There was no sign of any building.

Fatty looked and looked. That building, whatever it is, must be really well hidden, he thought. I wonder what it was used for in the last war. Some hush-hush stuff, I suppose. Well, it looks as if it's pretty hush-hush now, tucked away in this wood, guarded by this enormous wall and these gates. I wonder if they're locked.

He pushed against them. They didn't budge. The others tried too, but nobody could open them. Fatty thought they must be locked on the other side.

He glanced at the bell. Should he ring it? Yes, he would! He could always ask the way back to Peterswood, and make that the excuse for ringing.

Somebody at the little lodge nearby would probably answer.

So, to the others delight, Fatty pulled at the bell. A jangling noise came from above their heads, and they saw a bell ringing by one of the stone posts. Buster barked. He was startled by the bell.

'I'm going to ask the way,' said Fatty. 'We're lost. See!'

Somebody peered out of one of the little windows of the dark lodge. Then the door opened and a man came out. He was dressed like a gamekeeper, and had on a corduroy coat, trousers tucked into boots, and a belt round his waist. He looked surly and bad-tempered.

'What do you want?' he shouted. 'You can't come in here. Go away!'

Fatty promptly rang the bell again. Bets looked scared. The man came striding to the gates, looking black as thunder.

'You stop ringing that bell!' he shouted. 'What's the matter with you? This is private, can't you see that?'

'Oh!' said Fatty, looking innocently surprised. 'Doesn't my uncle, Colonel Thomas, live here?'

121

'No, he doesn't,' said the man. 'Go away, the lot of you, and take that dog with you.'

'Are you *sure* he doesn't live here?' persisted Fatty, still looking disbelievingly. 'Well, who does then?'

'Nobody! The house is empty, as anybody knows. And I'm here to see that kids and tramps don't get in and spoil the place, see? So get away quickly!'

'Oh – couldn't we just see round the garden,' begged Fatty, and the others, taking his cue, joined in. 'Yes, do let's, please!'

'I'm not going to stand here arguing all afternoon with a pack of silly kids,' said the man. 'You clear off at once. Do you know what I keep for people that come here and pry? I set my dogs on them.'

'Aren't you afraid of living here all alone?' said Bets, in an innocent voice.

'In one minute more, I'll open these gates and come out and chase you,' threatened the man – and he looked so terribly fierce that Fatty half-thought he might be as good as his word.

'Sorry to have bothered you,' he said, in his politest voice. 'Could you tell us the way back to Peterswood? We came over the fields, and we might lose our way going back. We haven't any idea where we are. What's this place called?'

'You just go and follow the lane, and you'll come to Peterswood all right,' said the man. 'And good riddance to you! Waking me up and bringing me out here for nothing. Be off with you!'

He turned to go back to his lodge. The children set off down the narrow track.

'What a very, very sweet-natured fellow,' said Larry, and they all laughed.

'Pity we couldn't get in,' said Pip in a low voice to Fatty. Fatty nudged him to keep quiet. Pip saw somebody riding up the track. It was a postman on his bicycle.

'Good afternoon,' said Fatty, at once. 'Could you tell us the time please?'

The postman got off his bicycle, undid his coat, and looked at his watch.

'Stopped!' he said. 'Don't know what the matter is with this old watch of mine. Just won't go now!'

'It's a nice old watch, isn't it?' said Fatty. 'Are you going up to those iron gates? We've just been there too, but the man at the lodge won't let us in.'

'He's the caretaker,' said the postman, buttoning up his coat. 'Proper bad-tempered fellow too.

Course he wouldn't let you in! He's there to stop children and tramps and trippers from spoiling the place. It belongs to an old fellow who won't live there himself, and asks such an enormous price for the place that nobody will buy it.'

'Really?' said Fatty with interest. 'Is he ever here?'

'Not that I know of,' said the postman. 'The only letters I ever take are for Mr Peters, the gatekeeper – the man you saw. He has too many for me! It's a job cycling out all this way each day to take letters to one man! Well – sorry not to be able to tell you the time. Bye-bye!'

He cycled off again, whistling. Fatty looked very pleased. 'Trust a postman to be able to tell you all you want to know!' he said in a low voice. 'A peculiar story, isn't it? A great big place, apparently unlet and empty, surrounded by an enormous wall, with one surly man to guard the place – and *he* receives a lot of letters! That last bit strikes me as mysterious.'

The children went down the lane, talking quietly. They all felt sure they had hit on their next mystery. But, so far, they couldn't make head or tail of it!

13. A LITTLE PORTRY

Ern was not told anything about the walk to the wood. He wanted to know, however, what were the steps that Fatty was going to take in the mystery of Christmas Hill.

'Well,' said Fatty, looking mysterious, 'word has come to me that a big robbery will be done in the next few days, and that the robbers on Christmas Hill will hide the loot in the old mill.'

Ern's eyes almost dropped out of his head. 'Coo!' he said, and couldn't say any more.

'The thing is – who's going to look for the loot after the robbery?' said Fatty seriously. 'I can't let any of the others, because they're forbidden to do things like looking for loot – and, at the moment, I've got other things in hand – tracking down the kidnappers, for instance.'

'Coo,' said Ern again, in awe. An idea shone brilliantly in his mind. 'Fatty! Why don't you let *me* find the loot? I could go and search the old mill for you. Lovaduck! I'd be awfully proud to find the swag.'

'Well – I *might* let you,' said Fatty. He turned to the others. 'What about it, Find-Outers? Shall we let him in on this and give him a chance of finding the loot? After all, he did a lot of hard work finding those clues.'

'Yes. Let him,' said the others generously, and Ern beamed and glowed. Whatever next! This was life, this was – creeping out at the dead of night – hunting for clues up on the hill next day – and now searching for hidden loot. What exciting lives the Find-Outers led!

Ern felt honoured to belong to their company. He felt he could write a 'pome' about it all. A line came into his head.

'The dire dark deeds upon the hill.' What a wonderful beginning to a 'pome'. Ern took out his portry notebook and wrote down the line before he could forget it.

'See that?' he said triumphantly to the others. '"The dark dire deeds upon the hill". That's the beginning of a new pome. That's real portry, that is.'

126

> *The dark dire deeds upon the hill*
> *Strike my heart with a deadly chill*

began Fatty.

> *The robbers rob and the looters loot,*
> *We'd better be careful they don't all shoot,*
> *They're deadly men, they're fearful foes,*
> *What end they'll come to, nobody knows!*
> *Oooh, the dark dire deeds upon the hill*
> *Strike my heart with a deadly chill!*

This poem was greeted with shrieks of delighted laughter by all the Find-Outers, even Buster joining in the applause. Fatty had reeled it off without stopping.

Only Ern didn't laugh. He listened solemnly, with open mouth, to Fatty's recitation, admiration literally pouring out of him.

'Fatty! You're a *real* genius. Why, you took my first line and you made up the whole pome without stopping. I'd never have thought of all that, if I'd sat down the whole day long.'

'Ah – that's the secret,' said Fatty wickedly.

'You don't sit down – you just stand up and it comes.
Like this.'

> Oh, have you heard of Ernie's clues,
> Ernie's clues, Ernie's clues,
> A broken lace, our Ernie found,
> A smoked cigar-end on the ground,
> A match, a packet, and a hanky,
> Honest truth, no hanky-panky!
> A rag, a tin, a pencil-end,
> How very clever is our friend!

Fatty couldn't go on because the others were
laughing so much. Ern was even more impressed.
But he felt down in the dumps too. He could never,
ever write pomes like that. How did Fatty do it? Ern
determined to stand up in his bedroom that night
when he was alone and see if portry rolled out of
him as it did out of Fatty.

'You're marvellous,' he said to Fatty. 'You ought
to be a poet, you really ought.'

'Can't,' said Fatty. 'I'm going to be a detective.'

'Couldn't you be both?' said Ern.

'Possibly, but not probably,' said Fatty. 'Not

worth it! Anyone can spout that sort of drivel.'

Ern was astonished. Could Fatty really think that was drivel? What a boy!

'Well, to come back to what we were talking about,' said Fatty, 'we've decided, haven't we, to let our Ern look for the loot?'

'Yes,' chorused everyone.

'Right,' said Fatty.

'When do I look for it?' said Ern, almost quivering with excitement. 'Tonight?'

'Well, it's not usual to look for loot before the robbery has been committed,' said Fatty, his face very serious. 'But if you think there's a chance of finding it before it's put there, you go on and do it, Ern.'

Bets gave a giggle. Ern worked all this out and blushed. 'Yes, I see what you mean. I won't go looking till after the robbery. But when will the robbery be?'

'The papers will tell you,' said Fatty. 'You look in your uncle's papers each morning, and as soon as you see that the robbery has been done, you'll know it's time to hunt in the old mill. And if you want to tell your uncle about it, we've no objection.'

'I don't want to,' said Ern. 'Well, I must be going. Lovaduck! You're a one for spouting portry, aren't you? I can't get over it. So long!'

He went, and the others began to laugh. Poor old Ern. He was a wonderful victim! Larry suddenly saw his 'portry notebook' left on the table.

'Hello! He's left this. Fatty, write something in it! Something about Mr Goon. Go on!'

'I'll write a "pome" about Mr Goon himself, in Ern's handwriting,' said Fatty, beginning to enjoy himself. He could imitate anyone's writing. Bets thought admiringly that there really wasn't anything that Fatty couldn't do – and do better than anyone else too! She stood close beside him and watched him.

He found a page in the book, and borrowed a pencil from Pip. 'Ern will be simply amazed to find a poem about his uncle written in his own book in his own handwriting,' said Fatty. 'He'll certainly think he must have written it himself – and he won't know when! Gosh, I wish I could be there when he finds it!'

He began to write. As usual the words flowed out straightaway. No puzzling his brains for Fatty, no

130

searching for a rhyme! It just came out like water from a tap.

TO MY DEAR UNCLE

Oh how I love thee, Uncle dear,
Although thine eyes like frogs' appear,
Thy body is so fat and round,
Thy heavy footsteps shake the ground.
Thy temper is so sweet and mild,
'Twould frighten e'en the smallest child,
And when thou speakest, people say,
'Now did we hear a donkey bray?'
Dear Uncle, how . . .

'Fatty! Ern's coming back!' said Bets suddenly. Her sharp ears had heard footsteps. 'Shut the book, quick!'

Fatty shut the book and slid it over the table. He picked up Buster and began to play with him. The others crowded round, laughing.

Ern's head came round the door. 'Did I leave my portry notebook here? Oh yes, I did. Silly of me. Good-bye all.'

He took his book and disappeared. 'What a pity you couldn't finish the poem, Fatty,' said Daisy. 'It was such a good one – especially all the "thees" and "thys". Just the kind of thing Ern would write.'

'And it was all in Ern's own writing too,' said Bets. She gave Fatty a hug. 'Fatty, you're the cleverest person in the world. How do you manage to copy other people's writing?'

'Just a gift!' said Fatty airily. 'I remember once last term we had to write an essay – and I wrote a very long one in my teacher's own handwriting. My word – you should have seen his face when I gave it in!'

'And I suppose, as usual, you got top marks for it?' said Pip, who only believed half of the extraordinary stories that Fatty told. As a matter-of-fact, most of them were perfectly true. The rest were almost true but rather exaggerated. Fatty certainly had a remarkable career at school, and had caused more laughter, more annoyance, and more admiration than any other boy there.

'I say, Fatty – poor old Ern may have to wait weeks to look for his loot,' said Daisy.

'No, he won't,' said Fatty. 'Haven't you noticed that there's a robbery reported nearly every day in the paper? It's about the commonest crime there is.

There'll be one tomorrow, or the next day, don't you worry.'

Fatty got out his own notebook, in which he kept particulars of whatever mystery the Find-Outers were trying to solve. He glanced down at his notes.

'This is a very difficult case,' he said to the others. 'There doesn't seem much we can do to find out anything. I've hardly got anywhere. I've found out that that building in the wood is called Harry's Folly, but nobody seems to know why. And the name of the man who is supposed to own it is Henry White – a very nice, common, insignificant name. I can't find out where he lives – all I've heard is that he lives abroad – which doesn't help us much!'

'We know that one of the men who was near the place was called Holland,' suggested Bets.

'Yes,' said Fatty, giving Bets a pat on the shoulder. 'That's a good point. I was just coming to that. As the men were walking, it looks as if they lived in or near Peterswood – though, according to Ern, they said goodnight to one another near him and went different ways. So it's likely that one might have been the caretaker, and the other was Holland. In which case, Holland was walking home.'

Everyone sat and thought. 'Where's your telephone directory, Pip?' said Fatty. 'Let's see if there are any Hollands in it.'

Pip fetched it. They all crowded round Fatty as he looked up the H's. 'Here we are,' he said. 'Holland. A.J. Holland. Henry Holland. W. Holland & Co, Garage proprietors, Marlow. Three Hollands.'

'Have to look them all up, I suppose,' said Larry. 'Lists of suspects! Three Hollands and one caretaker, called Peters!'

'Correct!' said Fatty. He looked thoughtfully at the directory. 'We'd better begin a bit of detecting again,' he said.

'Well, we're in on this,' said Larry at once. 'We *still* don't know if it's a mystery, so there's no harm in asking about the Hollands.'

'I believe my mother knows some people called Holland,' said Pip suddenly. 'I'll find out. Where do they all live, by the way?'

'Two in Peterswood, and the garage fellow at Marlow,' said Fatty. 'Well, Pip, you be responsible for finding out about one lot of Hollands. Larry and Daisy find out about the other – and I'll bike over to Marlow and smell out the Hollands there.'

They all felt very cheerful now that there was something definite to do. 'I think I'll go in disguise,' said Fatty, who always welcomed a chance to put on one of his disguises. 'I'll go as Ern! I bet I could make myself up to be exactly like him, now that I know him so well.'

'Why – you were quite annoyed with us for thinking Ern was you when we met him at the station,' said Daisy.

'I know. Still, I think I can put on a disguise that would deceive even old Mr Goon, if he wasn't too near!' chuckled Fatty. 'Well, Find-Outers, we'll do a spot of work tomorrow. Come on, Buster. Stop chewing the rug and come and have your dinner!'

14. SOME GOOD DETECTING

Quite a lot of things happened the next day. For one thing, there was the report of a big robbery in the daily papers. Ern could hardly believe his eyes when he saw the headlines! Fatty was right. There was the robbery. Coo!

Mr Goon was astonished to see Ern poring over the paper, reading details on the front page, and the back page too, quite forgetting his breakfast.

'What's up?' he said. 'Give me the paper. Boys shouldn't read at mealtimes.'

Ern handed it over, his head in a whirl. It had happened! The robbery was committed. Soon the loot would be in the old mill – and he'd find it. He'd be a hero. His uncle would admire him tremendously and be very sorry indeed for all the hard things he had said. Ern sat in a happy dream all through his breakfast, much to the surprise of his uncle.

Mr Goon read about the robbery too – but he

didn't for one moment think it had anything to do with Ern or himself. Robberies didn't concern him unless they were in his own district. He wondered why Ern looked so daft that morning. Had he found any more clues, or got any more news?

'No,' said Ern – he hadn't. He felt guilty when he remembered how he was going to find the loot, without telling his uncle anything about it – but he wasn't going to tell on Fatty any more. He was going to behave like a real Find-Outer!

The Find-Outers were busy that day. Pip and Bets had laid their plans very carefully, hoping not to arouse their parents' suspicions when they asked about the Hollands.

'We'll talk about people who have strange names,' decided Pip. 'I'll remind you of a girl you used to know whose surname is Redball – you remember her? Then you say "oh yes – and do you remember those people called Tinkle?" or something like that. And from that we'll go on to people with names of towns or countries – and when we get to the name Holland, I'll ask mother it she knows people of that name.'

'Yes, that would be a safe way of finding out,' said

Bets, pleased. So they began at breakfast time.

'Do you remember that girl you used to know – she had such a funny name,' said Pip. 'Redball, I think it was.'

'Oh yes,' said Bets. 'That *was* a funny name. I remember somebody else with a funny name too – Tinkle. Don't you remember, Pip?'

'Yes. It must be odd to answer to a name like that,' said Pip.

'You get used to it,' said his mother, joining in unsuspectingly.

'Some people have names of countries and towns,' said Pip. 'There's a composer called Edward Germany, isn't there?'

'Edward *German*,' corrected his father, 'not Germany. Plenty of people are called England and I have known an Ireland and a Scotland too.'

'Have you known a Holland?' asked Bets. This was going much better than they had hoped!

'Oh yes,' said Mrs Hilton at once. 'I know a Mrs Holland quite well.'

'Is there a Mr Holland?' asked Pip.

'Yes, I think so,' said Mrs Hilton, looking rather surprised. 'I've never seen him. He must be an old

138

man by now, because Mrs Holland is a very old lady.'

'Did they have any children?' asked Pip, ruling out old Mr Holland at once, because it didn't seem very likely that he would be engaged in any sort of mystery if he was so old.

'Well – their children would be grown up by now,' said his mother.

'Was there a boy?' asked Bets. 'A boy who would be a man now?'

Mrs Hilton felt surprised at these last questions. 'Why all this sudden interest in the Hollands?' she asked. 'What are you up to? You are usually up to something when you begin this sort of thing.'

Pip sighed. Mothers were much too sharp. They were like dogs. Buster always sensed when anything was out of the ordinary, and so did mothers. Mothers and dogs both had a kind of second sight that made them see into people's minds and know when anything unusual was going on. He kicked Bets under the table to stop her asking any more questions.

She understood the kick, though she didn't like it, and tried to change the subject. 'I wish I had another name, not Hilton,' she said. 'A more exciting name.

And I wish people would call me Elizabeth, not Bets.'

'Oh *no*,' said her father. 'Bets suits you. You are a proper little Bets.'

So the subject was changed and nothing more was said about the Hollands. But Pip and Bets were rather downcast because they hadn't found out what Fatty would want to know.

They went up to the playroom. Lorna, the maid, was there, dusting. 'It's a pity we didn't find out anything more about the Hollands,' said Bets. 'Oh – hello Lorna.'

'The Hollands?' said Lorna. 'What do you want to know about them for? There's not much to know! My sister works for old Mrs Holland.'

Well! Who would have thought that Lorna knew all about the Hollands! She told them in half a minute all they needed to know.

'Poor old Mrs Holland, she's all alone now that her husband's dead,' said Lorna. 'She had two daughters, but they're both living in Africa – and her son was killed in the last war. So she's nobody to care for her at all.'

Pip and Bets thought this was very sad. They also thought that their Mrs Holland, at any rate, didn't belong to the family of Hollands that Fatty was looking for.

'I wonder how Larry and Daisy are getting on,' said Pip.

They were getting on quite well! They had decided to ask their postman if he knew of any Hollands. He was a great friend of theirs. So they swung on their front gate that morning and waited till he came.

'Well, aren't you cold, out here so early?' said the postman when he came. 'Expecting something special?'

'Only our circus tickets,' said Larry truthfully. 'Ah – I bet they're in this envelope.'

He and the postman then had a very interesting talk about the various circuses they had both seen. 'Well, I must be off,' said the postman at last, and he turned to go.

As if he had only just thought of it, Larry called after him. 'Oh – half a minute – do you know anyone called Holland in Peterswood?'

'Holland – let me see now,' said the postman, scratching his rough cheek. 'Yes, there are two. One's in Rosemary Cottage. The other's in Hill House. Which one do you want?'

'One with a man in it,' said Daisy.

'Ah – then you don't want old Mrs Holland of Rosemary Cottage,' said the postman. 'Maybe you want the Hollands of Hill House. There's a Mr Holland there – but I did hear he's in America at the moment. Yes, that's right, he is. I keep taking postcards from America to the house for all the children. Five of them and little monkeys they are too!'

'Thank you,' said Larry, as a loud knocking came from behind him. It was his mother knocking on the window for them to come in to breakfast. He and Daisy fled indoors. It didn't look as if either of the Peterswood family of Hollands was the right one. Perhaps the Marlow Holland was the one they wanted!

Fatty was out on his bike when the other Find-Outers went to find him. 'Gone over to Marlow, I expect,' said Larry. 'Well, we'll wait for him. We'll wait in his shed.'

So they sat down in the cosy shed. Buster was not there. He had gone with Fatty, sitting upright as usual in Fatty's bicycle basket. Fatty had set off soon after breakfast before his mother could plan any jobs for him to do. It was not very far to Marlow – hardly three miles. The wind was cold, and Fatty's cheeks grew redder and redder.

He had made himself up just like Ern, enormous cap and all! Ern had teeth that stuck out, so Fatty had inserted his set of false celluloid teeth, which were very startling when displayed in a sudden grin. But they did make him look like Ern. He had put on a wig of rather untidy, coarse hair, very like Ern's, an old mac, and corduroy trousers. He wished the others could see him!

Buster was used to Fatty's changed appearances by now. He never knew when his master was going to appear as an old woman, a frail old man, an errand boy or a smart young man! But Buster didn't mind. Fatty always smelt the same, whatever he wore, so Buster's nose told him the truth, even if his eyes didn't.

Holland's garage was in a road off the High Street. Fatty cycled to find it. He saw it from a distance and then dismounted. Taking a quick look round to make sure that nobody saw him, he let all the air out of one of his tyres, so that the wheel bumped dismally on the ground.

Fatty then put on a doleful expression and

wheeled his bicycle to Holland's Garage. He turned in at the big entrance. There were a good many men working about on different cars, but nobody took any notice of him.

Fatty saw a boy about his own age washing down a car near the back of the garage. He went up to him.

'Hello mate,' he said, 'any chance of getting my bike mended here. Got a puncture.'

'Not just now,' said the boy. 'I do the punctures usually, but I'm busy.'

'Oh come on! Leave the washing alone, and do my bike for me,' said Fatty. But the boy was keeping an eye on a little window let into the wall of the wooden office near him. Fatty guessed correctly that the Boss might be in there.

'Can't do it yet,' said the boy, in a low tone. 'Hey, is that your dog in the basket? Isn't he good?'

'Yes. He's a fine dog,' said Fatty. 'Come on Buster, you can get down now!'

Buster leapt out of the basket, and ran to the hose. He barked at it and the boy gave him a spraying, which delighted Buster's heart.

'This is quite a big garage, isn't it?' said Fatty, leaning back against the wall. 'And a lot of men working in it. You must be pretty busy.'

'We are,' said the boy, still vigorously hosing the car. 'Busier than any other garage in the district.'

'I wouldn't mind taking a job in a garage myself,' said Fatty. 'I know a bit about cars. Any chance of a job here?'

'Might be,' said the boy. 'You'd have to ask Mr Williams there – he's the foreman. The Boss would want a look at you too.'

'Who's the Boss?' asked Fatty.

'Mr Holland, of course,' said the boy, his eye still on the window nearby. 'He owns this garage and another one some miles away. But he's usually here. Slave-driver, I call him.'

'Bad luck,' sympathized Fatty.

At that moment, another dog ran into the garage, and Buster darted at him. Whether Buster thought this was his own particular garage for the moment or not, Fatty didn't know – but Buster certainly acted as if he thought it was! Immediately a terrific howling, snarling and barking filled the place.

The little window near Fatty and the boy flew up at once. 'Who does that black dog belong to?' said a harsh voice.

'To this boy here, Mr Holland, sir,' said the garage boy, scared.

'What's your name?' demanded Mr Holland of Fatty, who was too surprised not to answer.

'Frederick Trotteville of Peterswood,' he said. 'What's the fuss about, sir?'

'I won't have dogs fighting in my garage,' snapped the man. 'I shall report your dog to the police if you bring him in here again. What have you come for? I've seen you chattering to this boy here for ages, making him do his work carelessly!'

'I came to ask if I could have my bike puncture mended,' said Fatty. He eyed Mr Holland, wondering whether to take a shot in the dark. He decided that he would.

'I want to ride over to a place called Harry's Folly, sir. It's got some fine iron gates, I'm told, and I'm interested in them, sir. Do you happen to know the best way to get to Harry's Folly?'

Fatty paused for breath, watching Mr Holland's face.

Mr Holland had certainly heard of Harry's Folly! He started a little when Fatty mentioned it, and a peculiar expression came over his face. Then his face smoothed out, and he answered immediately.

146

'Harry's Folly! No, I've never heard of it. We can't mend your bike here now. We're too busy. Clear off and take your dog with you.'

Fatty winked at the boy, who was now hosing the wheels of the car very, very well indeed. He called Buster. 'Hey, Buster! Come on!'

Buster left the fascinating hose and ran to Fatty's feet. Fatty wheeled his bike slowly out of the garage. He had a very satisfied expression on his face.

He was sure he had found the right Mr Holland! He had seen the little start the man gave at the mention of Harry's Folly. He knew the house all right – then why did he deny all knowledge of it?

'Very, very fishy,' decided Fatty, wheeling his bicycle into another side road. He pumped up the tyre swiftly, put Buster into the basket, and rode home, pleased with himself. Frederick Algernon Trotteville, you certainly are a good detective, Fatty told himself.

Back at the garage, Mr Holland sat in his office, quite silent. He took down a telephone directory and found the name Trotteville in it, and the address. He dialled a number and spoke to somebody.

'That you Jack? Listen – what was the name of

that kid who cleared up the missing necklace affair? Smart lad, you remember? Ah, I thought so. It may interest you to know he's just been here – complete with a dog called Buster – and told me he wanted to bike to a place called Harry's Folly! What do you make of that?'

Somebody evidently made a lot of it at the other end of the telephone, for Mr Holland listened intently for a few minutes. Then he spoke in a low voice, very near the mouthpiece.

'Yes, I agree with you. Kids like that must be dealt with. Leave it to me!'

15. MR GOON IS MYSTIFIED

Fatty cycled back to Peterswood, his mind hard at work. So Mr Holland was connected with Harry's Folly – and something was going on there, though Fatty couldn't imagine what! And Mr Holland didn't want people to know that he knew Harry's Folly – very peculiar altogether!

Shall I ring up Inspector Jenks? wondered Fatty. Or shall I just jog along on my own for a bit and try to solve the mystery? I'd like to do that. Funny to think of old Mr Goon getting all excited about an imaginary mystery, and here are the Find-Outers on the edge of a real one again!

He came to Peterswood. He stopped and put Buster down. The little Scottie bounded gleefully along by the bicycle.

In the distance, Mr Goon loomed up, on his way to talk severely to somebody who had let their chimney get on fire. To his enormous surprise, he saw somebody he thought was Ern riding a bicycle not far off. Mr Goon stopped and stared. He simply couldn't believe his eyes.

I left Ern at home, clearing out my shed, he thought. And I told him to clean my bike too. And now there he is, riding my bike, calm as a cucumber. I'll tell him off! Can't trust that boy at all, not for one minute!

He hurried towards Fatty. Fatty spotted him, and rode into a side street, waving merrily. He couldn't help hoping that Mr Goon would think he was Ern. Mr Goon, of course, hadn't any doubt of it at all. He was feeling very angry.

'Ern!' he called. 'ERN!'

Fatty took no notice, but rode slowly. Mr Goon hurried after him, his face going purple. That boy! Waving to him like that, cheeky as a monkey!

'ERN! YOU COME HERE!'

'Ern' rode round the corner and Mr Goon lost sight of him. He almost burst with rage. He retraced his steps and went back down the road, thinking of all the things he would do to Ern when he next saw him. To his astonishment, Ern actually appeared before him again, at the end of the street, and waved to him.

Mr Goon nearly had a fit. Fatty, of course, was dying of laughter at the sight of Mr Goon's face, and could hardly keep on his bicycle. He pedalled out of sight, tears running down his cheeks, almost helpless with laughter.

Once more he cycled round the block of houses and swam into Mr Goon's sight and out again. Mr Goon had now reached the pitch of shaking his fist and muttering, much to the amazement of all the passers-by. Fatty decided that he really would fall off his bicycle with laughter if he saw Mr Goon again, and regretfully pedalled home to tell the Find-Outers all that had happened.

But Buster, having spotted Mr Goon, thought it would be much more fun to trot at his heels than to go with Fatty. So he went behind him, sniffing at his trousers till the policeman felt him and turned in aggravation.

'Now you clear orf!' said Mr Goon exasperated. 'First it's Ern cheeking me, and now it's you! Clear orf I say, or I'll push you into the middle of next week.'

Buster didn't clear orf. He capered round Mr Goon, making playful little darts at his legs as if he wanted him to have a game. Mr Goon was so worked up that he backed straight into a street cleaner.

The street cleaner sent Buster away by frightening him with his broom. Buster trotted down the street pleased with himself. He certainly was a dog worthy of a master like Fatty!

Mr Goon finished his errand, gradually becoming less purple, and then walked home. Now to deal with Ern!

Ern had done a remarkably good morning's work. He had cleaned out the shed thoroughly, and now he was just finishing cleaning Mr Goon's bicycle. He was trying to think of some portry as he worked.

The next-door neighbour, Mrs Murray, thought that Mr Goon had a very hard-working boy for a nephew. Every time she hung out her washing, there he was, working away. She called over the fence.

'You're a good boy, you are! You haven't stopped working one minute since you began!'

Ern beamed. Mrs Murray went indoors. Mr Goon arrived, and walked down the little garden to where Ern was working by the shed, polishing the bicycle handles.

'Ho!' said Mr Goon, in an awful voice, 'so you thought you could tease me, did you? What do you mean by it, riding round the village on *my* bike, taunting me like that?'

Ern couldn't make out what his uncle was talking about at all. He stared at him, puzzled.

'What do you mean, Uncle?' he said. 'I've been here all the time. Look, the shed is clean and tidy – and I've almost finished your bike.'

Mr Goon looked. He was most surprised to see the shed so neat and tidy, and certainly his bicycle looked very spick and span.

'Ern, it's no good you denying it,' he said, his face going red, on its way to turning purple. 'I saw you – and you waved at me. I called you and you didn't come. What's more, you were riding my bike, and I don't allow that.'

'Uncle, I tell you, I've been here all morning,' said Ern, in an aggrieved voice. 'What's the matter with you? Haven't I done all you said? I tell you I didn't ride your bike. You've made a silly mistake.'

Mr Goon was now purple. He raised his voice. 'I won't have you cheek me, Ern, see? You were out on my bike, and you cheeked me? I tell you . . .'

Mrs Murray popped her head over the fence. She had heard everything, and she meant to put in a word for that hard-working boy, Ern.

'Mr Goon,' she said, and the policeman jumped. 'Mr Goon! That boy hasn't left this garden. A harder-working boy I never did see in all my life. You ought to be proud of a boy like that instead of accusing him of things he never did. I tell you, Mr Goon, that that boy hasn't budged from his place. I've been in and out with my washing, and I know. You leave that nephew of yours alone, or there's things I'll tell to everyone. Ah, you may be an officer of the law, Mr Goon, but you don't deceive *me*! I remember when . . .'

Mr Goon knew that there was absolutely no way of stopping Mrs Murray once she had begun. He was afraid of what she might say in front of Ern. So he put on a very dignified face, said 'Good morning to you, madam,' and marched indoors. Retreat was always the best policy when Mrs Murray was on the warpath!

'You stick up for yourself, lad,' said Mrs Murray. 'Don't you let him go for you like that!'

A voice bellowed from the kitchen. 'ERN!'

Ern dropped his duster and ran. However mistaken his uncle might be, he was still an uncle with a fierce temper and Ern thought he had better keep on the good side of both.

Mr Goon said no more about Ern riding his bike. An uncomfortable thought had come into his mind. He was wondering if that boy who looked like Ern could possibly have been Fatty up to his tricks. Ern must certainly have been in the garden all the time if Mrs Murray said so. Her tongue was sharp and long but it told the truth.

'Have you seen those kids today yet?' asked Mr Goon. 'Got any more news for me?'

'You know I haven't been out, Uncle. I've just told you so,' said Ern. 'I'd like to go and see them this afternoon though.'

Ern was longing to discuss the robbery with the Find-Outers. He had got the paper again as soon as his uncle had gone out, and read every single detail. The jewels those thieves had taken! Coo! There ought to be a fine bit of loot up at the old mill tonight! Ern was thrilled at the thought.

How that boy Fatty knows these things just beats me, thought Ern. He's a wonder, he is! I wish I could be like him. I'd do anything in the world for Fatty!

A good many people felt like that about Fatty. However annoying, boastful or high-handed he was, people always admired him and wanted to do things for him, especially other boys. He was head and shoulders above them in brains, boldness and courage, and they knew it.

Ern rushed round to the Find-Outers immediately after his dinner. They were at Fatty's, down in the cosy shed. He had been telling them all his adventures of the morning. They had admired the things he had found out at Holland's garage and had roared with laughter at the way he had played a trick on Mr Goon, pretending to be Ern.

'I expect Ern will be along soon,' said Fatty, opening a daily paper. 'Anyone see the account of this big robbery? Ern will be sure to think it's the one we meant!'

Larry and Daisy had seen it, but not Pip or Bets. They all pored over it, and Ern chose a very good moment to come into the shed.

'Hello!' he said, beaming round. 'Hey – you're looking at the story of the robbery! You're a marvel, Fatty, to know it was going to be done so soon. I can't think why you don't tell the police beforehand, when you know these things.'

'They wouldn't believe me,' said Fatty truthfully.

'Well, Ern – there should be plenty of fine loot up in the old mill soon!'

'I'm going tonight,' said Ern solemnly. 'It's awfully good of you to let me, Fatty.'

'Don't mention it,' said Fatty. 'Spleshure.'

'Pardon?' said Ern.

'SPLESHURE!' said Fatty loudly.

The others laughed. 'What's he say?' said Ern, puzzled.

'He means "It's a pleasure,"' explained Bets, giggling.

'Swatesaid!' chorused the Find-Outers together.

'Funny way of talking you have sometimes,' said Ern to Fatty, seriously. 'My uncle wasn't half strange with me this morning. Said he saw me riding his bike and taunting him when all the time I was cleaning out his shed.'

'Must be mad,' said Fatty. 'Well, Ern – the best of luck to you tonight. I hope the swag won't be too heavy for you to carry.'

'Coo!' said Ern, in alarm. 'I never thought of that!'

16. UNPLEASANT NIGHT FOR ERN

Ern passed the rest of the day in a state of excitement. His uncle couldn't think what was the matter with him.

'Thinking out some more of your wonderful portry, I suppose,' he said scornfully.

'No, I'm not,' said Ern, and he wasn't. He was thinking of what he was going to do that night. There would be a small moon. That would help him to find the way properly this time without making a mistake. Would the loot be too heavy? Well, if it was, he'd go twice to fetch it!

Ern went to bed early again. Mr Goon felt that something was up. Ern knew something that he hadn't passed on to his uncle. Drat the boy!

He listened at Ern's door when he went up to bed himself. If Ern was asleep, he'd creep in and get that notebook again. But Ern wasn't asleep. He was tossing and turning, because Mr Goon could quite well hear the bed creak.

Mr Goon undressed and got into bed, meaning to lie awake till Ern was asleep. But somehow he didn't. His eyes closed and soon Ern heard the familiar snores echoing through the little house.

Ern didn't want to go to sleep. He wanted to keep awake safely and leave for Christmas Hill about one o'clock when the moon would be up and giving a little light.

But it was hard to keep awake. Ern's eyes kept closing. He sat up straight. This wouldn't do. He'd be asleep in half a tick.

A thought came into his head. He remembered how Fatty had said that portry would come pouring out of you if you stood up to say it. It would be a good chance to try it now – Uncle was asleep – there was no one to interrupt him. And it would stop him dropping off to sleep.

Ern got out of bed. It was cold and he shivered. He pulled on his overcoat and put a scarf round his neck. He got out his portry notebook, and his book of clues and suspects. He was proud of them both.

He read down his list of clues again. Then he took a pencil and wrote a few lines on the next page.

> *Robbery committed January 3rd. Loot will*
> *be hidden in the old mill on Christmas Hill.*
> *Ern Goon detailed to find it on night of*
> *January 4th.*

That looked good. Ern drew a line under it and thought with pleasure of what he might be able to write the next morning. 'Loot collected. Worth about ten thousand pounds.' How he hoped he would be able to write that down too!

Now for the portry. He read through his various 'poems' and decided that they were not nearly as good as the ones Fatty had made up out of his head on the spur of the moment. He didn't see the one that Fatty had written in the book about Mr Goon. He didn't even know it was there.

Ern shut the portry notebook and put it on top of the other book. Then he stood up to begin saying portry straight out of his head like Fatty.

But somehow it wouldn't come. Ern stood there, waiting and shivering. Then suddenly a line came into his head. Ah – it was beginning!

Ern recited the line, '*The pore old man lay on the grass . . .*'

He stopped. Nothing else came. Now if only he were Fatty, he'd go on with another line and another and another – a whole poem, in fact, which he could remember and write proudly down.

He recited the line again, a little more loudly. '*The pore old man lay on the grass . . . on the grass . . . on the . . .*'

No, it wasn't any good. He couldn't think of another line to follow. But that was just it – Fatty didn't *have* to think. Portry just came out of him without stopping when he wanted it to! Perhaps Fatty was a genius and Ern wasn't. Ern thought sadly about this for a moment.

Then he began again, reciting loudly, '*A pore old man lay on the grass, A pore old man lay on the grass, A pore old man . . .*'

Mr Goon, in the next room, woke up with a jump. What was that peculiar noise? He sat up in bed. A voice came to him from the bedroom next to his. Mr Goon listened in amazement.

'*A pore old man lay on the grass, A pore . . .*'

'It's *Ern*!' said Mr Goon, really astonished. 'What's he doing, talking in the middle of the night about pore old men lying on grass? He must be out of his mind!'

Mr Goon put on a dressing-gown much too small for him and went majestically into Ern's room. The boy stood there in the dark, still reciting his one line desperately. *'The pore old man . . .'*

'Now what's all this?' said Mr Goon in a loud voice and Ern nearly jumped out of his skin. 'Waking me up with your pore old men! What do you think you're doing, Ern? I won't have this kind of behaviour, I tell you straight.'

'Oh, it's you, Uncle,' said Ern weakly. Mr Goon switched on the light. He saw Ern there in coat and scarf and he was even more astonished.

'You going somewhere?' he inquired.

'No. I was cold so I put some things on,' said poor Ern, getting into bed. 'I was only making up portry, Uncle. It comes better when you stand up.'

Mr Goon caught sight of the two notebooks on a chair. 'I'll teach you to wake me up in the middle of the night with portry!' he snorted, and picked up the two books to take back with him.

'Uncle! Oh Uncle, please don't touch those!' begged Ern, leaping out of bed and trying to take them from his uncle. But Mr Goon held them all the more tightly.

'What's the matter? What are you so upset about? I'm not going to throw them into the fire,' said Mr Goon.

'Uncle!' wailed Ern. 'They're private. Nobody is to read those but me.'

'Oh!' said Mr Goon. 'That's what *you* think!' and he switched off the light and shut the door. Ern got into bed, shivering with fright. Now his uncle would read about the loot – and the wonderful secret would be out! Ern shed a few tears onto the sheet.

Mr Goon read through the portry notebook first. When he came to the poem about himself he could hardly believe his eyes. How could Ern write such a rude poem? Downright rude, it was. Talking about his uncle's eyes in that way, and his voice – and that bit about the donkey's bray! Mr Goon felt himself swelling up with righteous rage.

He then read the other book. He only glanced at the clues and other notes which he had read before. But when he came to the bit Ern had written in that very night, his eyes grew rounder than ever.

Robbery committed January 3rd. Loot will be hidden in the old mill in Christmas Hill.

163

Ern Goon detailed to find it on night of
January 4th.

Mr Goon read this several times. What an extra-ordinary thing! What robbery? And how did anybody know where the loot was? And who told Ern to get it? That boy Frederick, of course! Mr Goon gave one of his snorts. Then he sat and thought very deeply.

It was a real bit of luck that he had got Ern's notebooks tonight! Now *he* could go and find the loot instead of Ern. That would be a bit of a blow to that boy Frederick! Aha! He wouldn't like Mr Goon turning up with the loot instead of Ern. And what would Inspector Jenks say to all this? He wouldn't be pleased with anybody but Mr Goon!

He read the bit of portry about himself again, and felt very angry indeed. Ungrateful boy Ern was! He determined to give Ern something to remember.

Ern heard Mr Goon go downstairs. He heard him come up again. He heard him open his door and switch on the light – and oh, what a horrible sight, there stood his uncle at the door, his face red and angry.

'Ern,' said Mr Goon in a sad voice, 'this is going to hurt me more than it hurts you. I've read that pome you wrote about me. It's wicked, downright wicked.'

Ern was astonished and alarmed. 'What pome, Uncle? I haven't written anything about you at all.'

'Now don't you go making things worse by telling stories,' said Mr Goon. He opened the portry notebook at the right page and, to Ern's consternation, he saw, written in his own handwriting, a poem addressed to 'My Dear Uncle'. He read it and quaked.

'Uncle! I didn't write it. I couldn't. It's too good a pome for me to write!'

'What do you mean, it's "*too good*"!' demanded his uncle. 'It's a wicked pome. And how you can sit there and tell me you didn't write it when it's in your own handwriting, well it beats me! I suppose you'll say next it isn't your writing?'

Ern looked at the 'pome'. 'It *is* my writing,' he said in a faint voice. 'But I don't understand it at all, Uncle, because honestly I don't remember writing it. I don't believe I *could* make up a pome as good as that. It's – It's like a dream, all this.'

'And there's another thing, Ern,' said Mr Goon, 'I've read what's in your other book too. That

165

robbery – and the loot hidden in the old mill. You never told me nothing about that, nothing at all. You're a bad boy. And bad boys get punished.'

Poor Ern! Mr Goon looked at him grimly. 'And don't you think you're going loot-hunting tonight, because you're not! I'm going to lock you in your bedroom, see? And you can just spend the night thinking of what happens to bad boys who write rude pomes and don't tell their uncle the things they ought to know!'

And with that, Mr Goon switched off the light, shut the door – and locked it! Ern's heart sank. Now he was properly done. No going up to the old mill for him tonight. A horrid thought struck his head under the pillow and he wept for his locked door, and his lost hopes.

He heard Mr Goon dress. He heard him go quietly out of the house. Ern knew he was going up to Christmas Hill. Now he'd find the loot! All Fatty's plans would come to nothing because of him, Ern Goon, and his silliness. Ern felt very small and very miserable.

Then a thought struck him. He remembered the rude 'pome' about his uncle. He got out of bed and switched on the light. His portry notebook was on the chair where his uncle had tossed it. Ern picked it up and found the page with rude 'pome' on it. *To My Dear Uncle*.

Ern read it through six times. He thought it was remarkably clever. And, yes, it certainly was in his own handwriting, though he couldn't for the life of him remember when he had written it.

'I must have done it in my sleep,' said Ern, at last. 'Geniuses do strange things. I must have dreamt it last night, got out of bed in my sleep, and written it down. Coo! Fancy me writing a good pome like that. It's wonderful! It's better than anything Fatty could have done. Perhaps I'm a genius after all!'

He got into bed again, and put his notebook under his pillow. He recited the poem several times. It was a pity it wasn't finished. He wondered why he hadn't finished it. Funny he couldn't remember doing it at all! It showed how his brain worked hard when he was asleep.

Ern didn't mind very much that his uncle was finding the loot. He was so very proud to think that he, Ern Goon, had written a first-rate pome – or so it seemed to Ern.

He fell asleep reciting the pome. He was warm and cosy in his bed. But Mr Goon was not. He was far up on Christmas Hill, looking for loot that wasn't there!

17. UNPLEASANT NIGHT FOR MR GOON

Mr Goon laboured up Christmas Hill in a cold wind. He kept a sharp eye for mysterious lights and noises and hoped fervently that cows and hens and cats wouldn't suddenly moo and cluck and yowl as they had done the time before.

They didn't. The night was very peaceful indeed. A little moon shone in the sky. No mysterious lights appeared. There were no noises of any kind except the little crunches made by Mr Goon's big feet on the frosty hillside.

The old mill loomed up, faintly outlined in the darkness by the moonlight. Mr Goon tred cautiously. If the loot was there, the robbers might be about also. He felt for his truncheon. He remembered the man who had attacked him the other night, and once more thought proudly how he had sent him flying.

Everything was quiet in the old mill. A rat ran across the floor and Mr Goon caught sight of its two eyes gleaming in the darkness. An owl moved up above, and then swept off on silent wings, almost brushing Mr Goon's face, and making him jump.

After standing quite still for some time to make sure there was nobody there, Mr Goon switched on his powerful torch. It showed a deserted, ruined old place, with holes in the roof and walls, and masses of old rubbish on the floor. There were holes in the floor too and Mr Goon decided that he had better move cautiously or his feet would go through a rotten board.

His torch picked out what looked like a pile of rotten old sacks. The loot might possibly be hidden under those! Mr Goon began to scrabble about in them, tossing them to one side. Clouds of dust choked him and a nasty smell rose around him.

'Pooh,' said Mr Goon, and sneezed. His vast sneeze echoed round the old mill and would certainly have alarmed any robber within half a mile. Fortunately for him, there was nobody about at all.

Mr Goon then began on a pile of old boxes. He disturbed a nest of mice, and made a few rats extremely angry. One snapped at his hand and Mr Goon hit at it with his torch. The torch missed the rat but hit the wall behind – and that was the end of the torch. It flared up once and then went out. No amount of shaking would make it light up again.

'Broken!' said Mr Goon, and hurled the torch at the wall in anger. 'Drat that rat! Now I can't see a thing.'

He had some matches in his pocket. He got them out and struck one. He saw some sacks in another corner. The match went out and Mr Goon made his way across the floor to the sacks. His foot sank into a hole in the boarding and he had a hard struggle to get it out again.

By this time Mr Goon was feeling so hot that he considered taking off his top-coat. He reached the sacks and began feeling about in them. Any cases of jewels? Any cash boxes? His fingers felt something hard, and his heart leapt. Ah – this felt like a jewel case!

He pulled the box out of the sacks. He opened it in the dark and dug his fingers in. Something sharp pricked him. Mr Goon lit a match to see what was in the box.

Rusty tacks and nails lay there, and Mr Goon felt his heart sink. Only an old box of nails! He licked his bleeding finger and thumb.

Mr Goon worked very hard indeed for the next hour. He went through all the piles of dirty, dusty old rags and sacks and newspapers. He examined every old or broken box, and put his hand down every hole in the wall, disturbing various families of mice but nothing else. He had a most disappointing night.

He stood up and wiped his hot face, leaving smears of black all across it. His uniform was cloudy with the old fine dust of the mill. He scowled into the darkness.

'No loot here. Not a sign of it. If that boy Frederick has been pulling Ern's leg about this, I'll – I'll – I'll . . .'

But before Mr Goon could make up his mind exactly what he would do to Fatty, a frightful screech sounded just above his head.

Mr Goon's heart stood still. The hair on his head rose up straight. He swallowed hard and stood absolutely still. Whatever could that awful noise be? Was somebody in pain or in terror?

Something very soft brushed his cheek and another terrible screech sounded just by his ear. It was more than enough for Mr Goon. He turned and fled out of the old mill at top speed, stumbling and almost falling as his foot caught in the rubbish lying around.

The screech owl saw him go, and considered whether to go after him and do another screech near his head. But the movement of a mouse down below on the floor caught his eye, and he flew silently down to catch it.

Mr Goon had no idea that the frightful noise had come from the screech owl that lived in the old mill. All kinds of wild ideas went through his mind as he stumbled down the hill, but not once did he think of the right one – the harmless old owl on the rafters in the ruined roof.

His heart beat fast, he panted loudly, and little drops of perspiration ran down his face. Mr Goon made up his mind very, very firmly that never again would he go looking for loot on Christmas Hill in the dark. He'd rather let Ern go, yes, a hundred times rather!

He calmed down a little as he reached the bottom of the hill. He had wrenched his right ankle and it made him limp. He thought of Ern safe in his warm bed and envied him.

He walked home more slowly, thinking hard. He

thought of the rude 'pome' in Ern's book. He thought of all the clues and other notes he had read. He marvelled that Fatty should have let Ern go to look for the loot – if there *was* any loot. That boy Frederick was always at the bottom of everything!

Mr Goon let himself into his house, went upstairs and switched on his bedroom light. He stared in horror at himself. What a sight he was! Absolutely filthy. His face was criss-crossed with smears of dirt. His uniform gave out clouds of dust wherever he touched it. What a night!

Mr Goon washed his face and hands. He took off his dirty uniform and put it outside on the little landing, because it smelt of the rubbish in the old mill. Ern found it there the next morning and was most astonished.

Mr Goon got into bed tired out, and was soon snoring. Ern was asleep too, dreaming that he was broadcasting his poem about Mr Goon. Lovaduck! Fancy him, Ern Goon, at the BBC!

In the morning, Ern was sulky because he knew that his uncle had gone off to get the loot. Had he found it? Would he tell him if he had? He had unlocked Ern's bedroom door though.

Mr Goon was late down for breakfast. He was feeling very, very tired. Also, in the bright light of morning, he couldn't help thinking that perhaps he had been rather foolish to rush off to Christmas Hill in the middle of the night like that. Loot in the old mill didn't seem nearly so likely now as it had seemed to him the night before.

Ern was eating his porridge when his uncle came down. They both scowled at one another. Ern didn't offer to get his uncle's porridge out of the pan for him.

'You get my porridge, and be quick about it,' said Mr Goon. Ern got up and mumbled, 'Can't do anything right for you. Serve you right if I ran away!'

'Gah!' said Mr Goon, and began to eat his porridge even more noisily than Ern.

'Locking me in my bedroom so that I couldn't do my bit,' went on Ern, sniffling. 'And *you* went off after the loot, so you can't pretend you didn't, Uncle. It was a mean trick to play. You wait till I tell the others what you did.'

'If you so much as open your mouth about anything I'll show you what I really *can* do!' said Mr Goon. 'You just wait.'

Ern sniffed again. 'I'll run away! I'll go to sea! That'll make you sorry you treated me so crooly!'

'Gah!' said Mr Goon again, and cut himself a thick slice of bread. 'Run away! Stuff and nonsense. A boy like you hasn't got the courage of a mouse. Run away indeed!'

Breakfast was finished in silence. 'Now you clear away and wash up,' said Mr Goon at the end. 'I've got to go out for the rest of the morning. You get that pot of green paint out of the shed and paint the fence nicely for me. No running round to those kids, see?'

Ern said nothing. He just looked sulky. Mr Goon, who had come down to breakfast in his dressing-gown, now put on his mackintosh and took his uniform into the garden to brush. Mrs Murray next door was amazed to see the clouds of dust that came out of it.

'Been hiding in a dustbin all night to watch for robbers?' she inquired, popping her head over the fence.

Mr Goon would have liked to say 'Gah!' but that kind of exclamation didn't go down very well with Mrs Murray. He just turned a dignified back and went on brushing.

Ern collected the dirty breakfast things and took them into the kitchen to wash. He brooded over his wrongs. Uncle was hard and unkind. Ern had hoped to have such a wonderful time with Mr Goon, and had actually meant to help him with his 'cases' – and all that had happened was that he was always getting into some kind of trouble with his uncle. There was no end to it.

'As soon as he's gone out of the house, I'll pop round to Pip's,' thought Ern. 'The Find-Outers said they'd be there. I'll tell them about last night and how Uncle locked me in. And I'll show them that wonderful pome. They'll be surprised to think I can do things like that in my sleep. I hope Fatty won't be cross because I couldn't go and look for the loot.'

Mr Goon went off on his bicycle at last. Ern slipped out of the back door and made his way to Pip's. With him he took his portry notebook. He read the rude pome again and again and marvelled. 'I reely am a genius!' he thought, proudly. 'That's a wonderful pome even if it's rude.'

18. THINGS HAPPEN TO ERN

There was nobody in Pip's playroom except Bets. She had a cold and was not allowed out. The others had gone on an errand for Pip's mother.

'Hello!' said Bets. 'How did you get on last night, Ern? Did you find the loot?' She giggled a little as she asked Ern. Poor Ern! Had he gone loot-hunting all by himself? What a simpleton he was!

Ern sat down and poured out all the happenings of the night before. Bets soon grew serious as she heard how Mr Goon had punished poor Ern. Bets was very tender-hearted and could never bear anyone to be punished.

'Oh, Ern, poor Ern! That horrid, hateful Mr Goon!' she said, and Ern glowed at having so much sympathy. He thought Bets was the nicest little girl he had ever met.

'You're nice,' he said to Bets. 'I wish you were my sister. I bet Sid and Perce would like you too.'

Bets felt very guilty when she thought of all the tricks that the Find-Outers had played on Ern. She wished they hadn't now. Especially that poem trick! It was that poem, written in Ern's own handwriting by Fatty that had made Mr Goon so angry with Ern. Oh dear! This was dreadful. They would have to own up to Ern and to Mr Goon too. Fatty would hate that – but they couldn't go on deceiving Ern like that.

Ern opened his portry notebook. 'You know, Bets,' he said, 'I don't remember writing this pome at all. That's funny, isn't it? But it's a wonderful pome and I'm really proud of it. It was worth a scolding! Bets, do you think I can possibly be a genius, even a little one, if I can write a pome like that and not know I'd written it? I must have done it in my sleep.'

Bets didn't know what in the world to say. She looked at Ern's serious face. Ern began to read the pome in a solemn voice, and Bets went off into giggles. She really couldn't help it.

'Don't you think it's a wonderful pome, Bets?' said Ern, hopefully. 'Honestly, I didn't think I could write one like that. It's made me feel all hopeful, like.'

'I don't wonder it made your uncle angry,' said

179

Bets. 'Poor Ern. Now wouldn't you like to go and meet the others? They've gone to Maylins Farm for Mummy. You'll meet them coming back if you go now.'

'Right,' said Ern, getting up. He put his precious notebook into his coat pocket. 'Do you think Fatty will be annoyed about me not going to find the loot?' he asked anxiously.

'Oh no. Not a bit,' Bets assured him. Ern grinned at her, put on his coat and started off downstairs. He saw Mrs Hilton crossing the hall below and waited till she had gone and then darted out of the house.

He made his way through the village, keeping a sharp eye out for his uncle. He went up the lonely lane that led to Maylins Farm. It was a long and winding road, with few houses. Ern went along with his head down, muttering the first line of a new pome he was thinking of.

'The pore little mouse was all alone . . .'

A car came down the lane. Ern looked up. A man was at the wheel, and another man at the back. Ern stood aside to let the car pass.

It went on a few yards and stopped. The man at the back leaned forward and said something to the driver. The driver opened his window and shouted back at Ern.

'Hey, boy! Do you know the way to the post office?'

'Yes,' said Ern. 'It's down there a little way. Turn to the left, up the hill a little way, and you'll see a . . .'

'Jump in and show us, there's a good lad,' said the driver. 'Save us a lot of time. We've lost the way two or three times already. Here's some money if you'll help us.'

He held out some coins and Ern's eyes brightened. He only had a small amount of pocket money and this seemed like riches to him. He hopped in beside the driver at once. The man at the back had his face buried in a newspaper.

The car started off again – but instead of going off at the turning to the post office it swept on past it, took a left-hand turn and then a right-hand one, and then shot off at a great speed towards Marlow.

Ern was astonished. 'Here! This isn't right!' he said. 'Where you going?'

'You'll see,' said the man at the back, in a nasty sort of voice that sent a horrid little thrill down Ern's spine. 'We're going to show you what we do with interfering boys.'

Ern stared at the two men in alarm. 'What do you mean? What have I interfered in? I don't understand.'

'You soon will,' said the man at the back. 'Always poking your nose into this and that, aren't you, Frederick Trotteville? You thought when you came along to the garage the other day you were being very clever, didn't you?'

Ern simply couldn't make head or tail of what the sour-faced man at the back was saying. He felt very frightened.

'I'm not Frederick,' he said. 'I'm Ern Goon. My uncle is the policeman at Peterswood.'

'Don't waste your breath telling those tales to us,' said the driver grimly. 'Trying to be so innocent! You certainly *look* a simpleton – but you can't put it across us that you are. We know you all right.'

Ern gave up. What with mysterious, rude pomes, a furious uncle, and now two men kidnapping him, he simply didn't know what to think!

Kidnappers! At that thought poor Ern shivered and shook. Fatty had said there were two gangs – one gang was kidnappers, the other robbers. Now he had got mixed up with the kidnappers! This was a simply frightful thought.

He didn't know why the men thought he was Fatty. But they, of course, had only seen Fatty disguised as Ern, the day he had cycled over to Holland's garage. When they had spotted the real Ern wandering up the lane, they had had no doubt that it was Fatty, the same boy they had seen with the dog at the garage.

Ern was taken to a garage some miles from Marlow, owned by Mr Holland. He was driven into a big shed, and made to get out. A door led from the shed up a ladder into a small room. The men pushed Ern there.

'If you shout you'll get a hiding,' said Mr Holland. You'll be here all day and if you're quiet you'll get food and drink. If you're not, you won't. We're going to take you somewhere else tonight where you can have a nice quiet time all by yourself till we decide what to do with you. It's time silly kids like you were stopped from poking your noses into other people's business.'

Ern was completely cowed. He sat down on some straw in the tiny room, and trembled till the men had gone out of the door and locked and bolted it. He looked for a window but there was none. The only light came in through a tiny skylight set in the roof.

Ern began to sniffle. He was no hero, poor Ern, and things were happening too fast for him. He sat there all morning, miserable and frightened.

The door was unbolted and unlocked at half past one, when Ern had begun to fear that he was going to be starved. A hand came in with a loaf of bread, a jar of potted meat and a jug of water. Nothing else. But Ern was so hungry that he ate the whole loaf, and the potted meat too, and drank the last drop of the water.

He was given no tea. At half past four, when it was almost dark, the door opened again and the men came in. 'Come on out,' said one of them. 'We're going.'

'Where to?' stuttered Ern, afraid.

There was no answer. He was pushed down the ladder, into the shed, and into the back of the car. The two men got in at the front. The car backed out.

Ern was in despair. How could he let the others know anything? He felt sure that if he were Fatty he would be able to find some way of telling the Find-Outers that something dreadful had happened to him.

He felt in his pocket. His clues were still there, all ten of them. Suppose he threw them out of the window one by one? There *might* be a chance of one of the Find-Outers picking one of them up. They would recognise a clue immediately.

It was a very faint hope indeed, especially as Ern had no idea where the car was going. He might be miles away from Peterswood. He peered out of the window to see if he could recognise anything at all in the darkness.

No, there was nothing to tell him where he was. But, wait a bit – wasn't that the post office in Peterswood? Yes, it was! They were actually going through Peterswood! Ern wondered if he could let down the window far enough to throw out his clues one by one. He tried, but at once one of the men turned round.

'Don't you dare try to open the window! If you think you're going to shout, you can think again!'

'I'm not going to,' protested Ern. Then a really brilliant idea struck him. 'I feel sick, see? I want air. Let me open the window a few inches. If you don't, I'll be sick all over the car.'

The man gave an impatient exclamation. He

leaned back and opened the window about two inches. Ern made a horrible noise as if he was on the point of being violently sick. He felt very clever indeed. The man opened the window a little more.

'If you dare to be sick in the car I'll box your ears!' he threatened.

Ern made a noise again, and at the same time threw out the button with the bit of cloth attached. Then he threw out the cigar-end. Next went the pencil stub with E.H. on the end and then the rag.

Every now and again, Ern made a horrible noise and the man glanced back anxiously. They were nearly there! That wretched boy. Mr Holland made up his mind to give him a good spanking if he spoilt the car.

Out went the next clue – the hanky with 'K' on. Then the broken shoelace – then the empty cigarette packet. After that the tiny bit of paper with the telephone number went fluttering into the road, and then the rusty old tin. That was the lot.

Ern leaned back, feeling pleased. Aha! The clues he had found on Christmas Hill were going to be first-rate clues as to his whereabouts for all the Find-Outers. Ern was quite certain that people as clever as the Five Find-Outers would somehow find the clues and read them correctly.

The man looked round. 'Feel better?' he said.

'I'm all right now,' said Ern, and grinned to himself in the darkness. He *was* clever! He was surprised himself to think how clever he was. The man shut the window up again. The car was going slowly now, up a very narrow lane. The headlights were out. Only the sidelamps were on.

The headlights were flashed once as they came round a bend. The car slowed. Ern tried to see why but he couldn't. There came the creak and clang of gates, and the car moved on. It ran on to something smooth after a short while and stood still. Then, to Ern's terrific alarm, the car suddenly shot straight downwards as if it were a lift! Ern clutched the sides and gasped.

'Here we are,' said Mr Holland's voice. 'Out you get, Frederick Trotteville. This is the place you were inquiring about – but you'll soon wish you had never never heard about it in your life! Welcome to Harry's Folly!'

19. MR GOON FEELS WORRIED

The Find-Outers were very surprised when they got back to Bets, to hear that Ern had been sent to meet them.

'We never saw a sign of him,' said Fatty. 'I suppose he went home after all.'

They listened to Bets' account of what Ern had told her of the night before. Their faces became serious. It was one thing to pull Ern's leg to get a laugh out of him. It was quite another to cause him to get into trouble.

'Golly! And old Mr Goon went loot-hunting on Christmas Hill instead of Ern. Won't he be wild when he knows it was a put-up job?' said Larry.

'We'll have to tell Ern – and Mr Goon too – that I wrote the poem,' said Fatty. He looked uncomfortable. 'Mr Goon will be furious. I shall get into a fine old row.'

'Yes, you will,' said Pip. 'He'll go round complaining again.'

'Ern was terribly terribly proud of the poem,' said Bets. 'He said that was the only thing that comforted him last night – the thought that he had written a wonderful poem like that, and hadn't even known he had. He thought he must have written it in his sleep. I simply couldn't bear to tell him he hadn't written it, Fatty.'

'It's a bit of a tangle, isn't it?' said Daisy. 'In order to make Mr Goon realise that he's treated Ern unfairly, we've got to disappoint Ern by telling him the poem isn't his! Poor old Ern! I wish we hadn't pulled his leg so much. He's awfully silly, but he's quite harmless and sometimes very nice.'

'An awful coward though,' said Pip. 'Look how he keeps giving everything away! It's a good thing it wasn't a *real* mystery we set him on. He'd have given absolutely every single thing away to Mr Goon.'

'Yes. He can't really be trusted,' said Daisy. 'But I do feel sorry about this. I wonder what's happened to him now. I suppose he went home.'

But Ern hadn't gone home, as we know. He didn't appear at dinnertime, and Mr Goon, who had got quite a nice dinner of stew and dumplings, felt most annoyed.

That pestering boy! He hadn't painted the fence green as he had been told to. Now he was late for dinner.

'Well, I shan't wait – and if he doesn't come, I'll eat the lot!' said Mr Goon. 'That'll learn him!'

So he ate the lot, and felt so very full afterwards that he sat down in his armchair by the kitchen fire, undid a few buttons, and immediately fell sound asleep. Mr Goon was tired after his night's hunting up on Christmas Hill. He slept and he slept. He slept the whole afternoon away. He didn't even hear the telephone ringing. He slept solidly all through the rrrrr-ring, rrrr-ring, his snores almost drowning the bell.

He awoke at half past five. He yawned, sat up, stretched, and looked at the clock. He looked again. What! Almost half past five! The clock couldn't be right! Mr Goon took out his big watch and looked at that too. Why, that said the same!

'I've been asleep three solid hours!' said Mr Goon, quite shocked. 'Shows how tired I was. Where's Ern? Why, he's almost let the fire out, and there's no kettle boiling for tea!'

He gave a loud yell, 'ERN! ERN!'

No Ern came. Mr Goon frowned. Where was that boy? He hadn't come in to dinner! Now he hadn't come in to tea. Gone round to those kids, he supposed, and they'd kept him for meals. Spun a wonderful tale about his crool uncle! Ho, Mr Goon would have something to say about that.

Mr Goon made himself a cup of tea very quickly. He didn't stop for anything to eat. He suddenly remembered that he was supposed to go along to Miss Lacey's and hear about two of her hens being stolen. How could he have forgotten that? If he'd gone about half past four, he could have had tea in the kitchen with Mrs Tanner, the cook. Fine gingerbread she made every week, as Mr Goon very well knew.

Mr Goon went off to Miss Lacey's. She was out. Mrs Tanner the cook told Mr Goon that Miss Lacey was annoyed because Mr Goon hadn't come along sooner. So the policeman didn't have a chance to sit in a warm kitchen and have a piece of new gingerbread. He was most annoyed, and went pompously down the steps into the darkness of the drive.

He wondered again where Ern was. Bad boy to stay away like that. Pretending he had run away perhaps! Mr Goon gave a small snort. Ern would never have the spunk to do a thing like that.

But a very small doubt crept into his mind at that moment. Suppose Ern really *had* run away? No, no, how silly! He must be somewhere with those kids.

Mr Goon walked up the road that led to the post office. It was dark and he shone his torch on the ground before him. It suddenly picked up something in its beam. A button!

Mr Goon always collected any button or pin he found. He picked this button up. It had a bit of cloth attached to it. Why – he knew that button and bit of cloth! It was one of Ern's clues!

So Ern's been along this way, thought Mr Goon. He picked it up. What's Ern doing, chucking his clues about like this? Ah – here's a pencil end! I bet it's the clue he found with E.H. at the end. Yes, it is!

He missed the rag, which had blown under the hedge. He walked on some way and saw a ragged handkerchief. He had a feeling it would have 'K' on. So it had. Another of Ern's clues. How extraordinary, thought Mr Goon. Then an idea came into his head.

It's those kids again, playing a trick on me! They've spotted me walking down here, and they've got Ern to chuck down his clues to lead me on! They'll jump out at me round the corner or send that pestering dog round my ankles. Well, I'm not going any further! I'm going straight round to Mr and Mrs Hilton to complain!'

Mr Goon made his way to Pip's house, filled with indignation. Getting Ern to throw down clues like that to lead him up the way just for a trick! What did they take him for?

Mr and Mrs Hilton were out. 'But the five children are here,' said Lorna, the maid. 'If it's them you're wanting to see, sir?'

'I'll see them,' said Mr Goon. 'You go up the stairs first and tell Trotteville to keep his dog under control. Nasty, snappy little beast that is.'

When Lorna appeared with her news, the Find-Outers looked surprised and Bets felt alarmed. Oh dear – what had happened now?

Mr Goon walked in. He put down the clues on the table. 'Another of your silly tricks, I suppose?' he said, glaring round. 'Getting Ern to chuck these about where you knew I'd find them. Ho – very childish, I must say!'

The Five Find-Outers gazed at the clues and

recognised them. Fatty picked up the button. He was puzzled.

'Where is Ern?' he asked Mr Goon. 'We haven't seen him all day.'

Mr Goon snorted. 'Think I believe that? Well, *I* haven't seen him all day either! But I bet he's hidden in this house somewhere! That's called aiding and abetting somebody, see?'

Fatty thought Mr Goon was being rather silly. 'Mr Goon, we – have – NOT seen Ern since early this morning when he came along here for a few words with Bets. Where *is* he?'

Mr Goon began to feel slightly alarmed. There was a ring of truth in Fatty's voice. If these kids hadn't seen Ern all day, where *was* he then? Surely he couldn't have run away? No, that wouldn't be in the least like Ern.

He stared at the silent children. 'How do *I* know where that dratted boy is?' he said, raising his voice a little. 'Worries the life out of me, he does – and you do your best to do the same. And let me tell you, *I* know all about this mystery of yours! Yes, I know more about robbers and kidnappers on Christmas Hill than *you* do!'

'I'm so glad to hear it,' said Fatty, in the very polite voice that made Mr Goon go purple. 'Perhaps you can solve it more quickly than we can. The thing is – where is Ern? He was very upset when he saw Bets this morning. Apparently you punished him last night, Mr Goon.'

Mr Goon could hardly speak. Then he stuttered with outraged feelings. 'Me! I never heard of such a tale. I gave him a scolding, see, for being rude.'

'Well,' said Fatty, and hesitated. Should he tell Mr Goon now about the poem – that *he* had written it and not Ern? No, perhaps it would be best to tell Ern first. But where *was* Ern?

Fatty felt really puzzled. The things Mr Goon had put on the table were certainly Ern's clues – the things he had picked up on Christmas Hill. They were not all there though. Fatty inquired about the rest.

'Didn't you find any more clues, Mr Goon? Are those all you picked up?'

'I don't know how many more you told Ern to put down for me to follow,' snorted Mr Goon. 'But I wasn't going to go wandering over half the town to find any more!'

'Where did you find these?' asked Larry.

'As if you didn't know!' said Mr Goon sarcastically. 'Where you put them, of course – or where you told Ern to put them. Up Candlemas Lane.'

'What could Ern have been doing there?' wondered Bets.

'Don't you really know where Ern is?' said Mr Goon, after a pause. Another little doubt was creeping in on him. Wouldn't it be awkward if Ern *had* run away because he, Mr Goon, had punished him? Perhaps he had gone home to his mother. Mr Goon decided to make inquiries when he got back, and find out. He could ring up a friend of his who knew Ern's mother, and get him to slip round quietly to Ern's home and find out if he was there.

'No. We don't know where he is,' said Fatty impatiently. 'Haven't we kept telling you that? I shouldn't be surprised, Mr Goon, if poor old Ern hasn't run away to sea or something, after your cruelty to him last night.'

Mr Goon, for once, had nothing whatever to say. Fatty's suggestion, coming on top of his own fear that Ern might have run away, made him quite tongue-tied. It was all very, very awkward. He began to wish he hadn't scolded Ern the night before.

He went soon after that, much to Pip's relief. He and Bets were afraid that their parents might arrive home before Mr Goon left, and they didn't want that to happen.

'It's very odd,' said Fatty, letting Buster off the lead, where he had held him tightly for the last quarter of an hour. 'We haven't seen Ern at all today. Only Bets saw him this morning. And now here's this tale of clues scattered about in Candlemas Lane. Why should Ern do that?'

'Hole in his pocket,' suggested Pip.

'Not very likely,' said Fatty.

'Perhaps he got tired of his clues and just *threw* them away,' said Bets.

'Silly idea,' said Pip scornfully.

'I'm going out with my torch to see if there are any more of Ern's clues scattered about,' said Fatty. 'I feel as if there's something wrong somewhere. I'm worried about our Ern!'

He went off by himself with Buster, his torch shining its beam in front of him. He made his way to Candlemas Lane.

He saw nothing in the way of clues at first – but further on, at the turning out of the lane into the track that ran across the fields for a mile or two to Harry's Folly, Fatty found three or four more of the clues. He stood thoughtfully in the track, puzzling things out in his mind. Where was Ern? What in the world could have happened to him?

20. FATTY ON THE TRACK

Ern didn't come home that night. By the time nine o'clock came, Mr Goon had worked himself into a terrible state of mind. He imagined all kinds of things happening to Ern. He had been run over. He had run off to sea and was already on a ship, being very seasick. He had gone home to his mother, and Sid and Perce, and told terrible tales about his uncle. All these things and many others flashed through Mr Goon's worried mind.

He tried to find out if Ern had gone home, but no, he wasn't there. Whatever was Mr Goon to do! He felt terribly guilty now. He, Ern's uncle, had driven him away! What would people think?

I'll stay up till eleven to see if Ern comes, thought Mr Goon. I'll put some bacon and eggs ready to cook for him when he comes – and I'll heat up some cocoa. I'll go and put a hot water bottle in his bed.

Mr Goon felt quite sentimental about Ern as the night wore on, and no Ern appeared. He remembered all Ern's good points and forgot the bad ones. He felt ashamed when he remembered how he had scolded Ern and locked him in.

Oh Ern, you come back and we'll get on fine, thought Mr Goon over and over again. Eleven o'clock struck. Mr Goon made up the fire again. Then he settled down in the armchair. He would wait up for Ern all night.

But suppose he didn't come? Mr Goon considered this with a very serious face. He'd have to ring up Inspector Jenks and report his disappearance – and the first question asked would be, 'Was the boy in any trouble before he disappeared?' And what was Mr Goon to say to that?

He fell asleep about midnight. He slept soundly through the night, and awoke in the morning, very cold and stiff, with the fire out – and no Ern anywhere! And now Mr Goon really did begin to feel frightened. Something *had* happened to Ern!

The telephone rang, and Mr Goon almost jumped out of his skin. He went to answer it. It was Fatty, asking if Ern had come back.

'No,' said Mr Goon. 'He hasn't. Have you heard anything about him?'

'Not a word,' said Fatty. 'It's pretty serious this, Mr Goon. Looks as if your telling-off has sent him away.'

Mr Goon was too upset even to get angry over Fatty's persistence in mentioning the scolding. 'What am I to do?' he said, in a dismal voice. 'You might not think it, Frederick Trotteville, but I'm very fond of Ern.'

'You hid your affection very well then,' came Fatty's smooth voice over the telephone. Mr Goon shook his fist at the receiver. That dratted cheeky boy! But the policeman soon forgot his anger in his worries about Ern.

'I'd better go to Inspector Jenks, I suppose,' said Mr Goon, after a pause. 'Trotteville, do you think this here mystery on Christmas Hill's got anything to do with Ern's disappearance? These kidnappers and whatnots?'

'You never know,' said Fatty, in a serious voice. 'Er – did you find the loot the other night, Mr Goon?'

'That's none of your business,' said Mr Goon, shortly. 'Well – I suppose I'd better go and see the Inspector.'

'Mr Goon, I don't know if you'd like to wait till tonight,' said Fatty suddenly. 'I've got an idea at the back of my mind which might just be the right one. But I can't tell you any more than that. It's *possible* I should be able to tell you where Ern is if you would like to wait another day before reporting that he's vanished.'

Mr Goon was only too glad to clutch at any straw. He was dreading having to go to the Inspector. He didn't want to say how he'd punished Ern the night before he went – nor did he want to say anything about the rude 'pome'. Why, the Inspector might even want to read it! Mr Goon's face burned at the very thought.

'Right,' said Mr Goon. 'I'll wait another day. I'll wait up tonight till I hear from you. Poor Ern – I do hope he's all right.'

'I'll give you a ring on the phone tonight, as soon as I know anything,' said Fatty.

He rang off. He was at his own house, and the Find-Outers were due down at the shed any moment. Fatty went with Buster down the garden, just in time to see the others coming in.

'No Ern yet,' he said. 'Mr Goon's getting all

worked up about him. And so he should! He doesn't like the thought of having to go and tell the Inspector how he scolded him in the middle of the night!'

'What *has* happened to Ern?' said Pip. 'I could hardly get to sleep last night for worrying about him – and thinking about those clues Old Clear-Orf found in Candlemas Lane.'

'I found some more last night,' said Fatty. 'And two of them were along the track that leads across the field to Harry's Folly! I believe Ern's there.'

'But why? Do you mean he went off across the fields to explore Harry's Folly or something?' demanded Larry. 'But he doesn't know anything about *that* mystery!'

'I know he doesn't,' said Fatty. 'All the same, I think he's there. I think he must have been *taken* there, but I can't imagine why. Even if Mr Holland came along in his car and saw Ern, why should he take him away?'

'I expect he thought Ern was *you*,' said Bets suddenly. 'After all, you were disguised as Ern when you went over there, weren't you? – and you *might* have given the game away to him, Fatty, when you mentioned Harry's Folly. He might have been scared, thinking you knew something, and decided to capture you!'

Fatty stared at Bets, thinking hard. Then he banged the table and made them all jump. 'That's it. Bets has got it! They've kidnapped Ern thinking he is me – and they think I know too much about Harry's Folly, because I spoke about it as I did! Good old Bets. She's the best Find-Outer of the lot!'

Bets was thrilled at this unexpected praise. She blushed red. 'Oh – we'd all have thought of it soon!' she said.

'Yes – Bets is right. They must have mistaken Ern for me – and – and – yes, I wonder if Ern could have thrown away those clues to warn us something was up – even to show us the way to follow?'

'That's too clever a thing for Ern to do,' said Daisy.

'Yes. It is a bit clever,' said Fatty thoughtfully, 'but in desperation Ern might be cleverer than he usually is. Tell me, Bets – what time did Ern leave you?'

'About half past ten,' said Bets. 'He said he was going off to meet you straightaway. He should have met you coming back about three-quarters of the way there.'

'I'm going out to make a few inquiries,' said

Fatty. 'Stay here, all of you. I'll be back.'

Fatty went into the village, and then turned up the way to Maylins Farm. He saw a small girl swinging on a gate and called to her.

'Hello Margery. Did you see Ern Goon here yesterday? You know Ern, don't you? The policeman's nephew.'

'Yes,' said Margery. 'I saw him going up this way yesterday morning. He didn't see me because I was hiding.'

'Did you see him come back again?' asked Fatty. 'You saw us all walking back, didn't you, later on? Did you see Ern again?'

'No, I didn't,' said Margery. 'There was a big car came down a little while after, and nearly knocked me over. Then you came with the others. That's all. What's Ern done?'

'Nothing,' said Fatty. 'Here's a pound. Catch!'

He walked on up the road thinking hard. Ern had gone to meet them up there – but hadn't come back. But a car had come along soon after. Was it Mr Holland's car, cruising round to snoop for Fatty perhaps – and finding Ern instead, thinking *he* was Fatty?

Some way up, in a very lonely part of the road, Fatty saw where a car had suddenly put on its brakes and swerved a little to a quick stop. He looked at the marks on the road thoughtfully, his mind working. This was probably where the men in the car had met Ern, thought he was Fatty, stopped suddenly, asked Ern some question to get him into the car – and gone off with him.

The car wouldn't go to Harry's Folly in the daytime, that was certain. It was more likely it would have gone to Marlow or to the other garage Mr Holland owned. The men would have locked Ern up somewhere for the day – and then perhaps they would have brought him back to Harry's Folly.

'And when Ern saw he was going through Peterswood he suddenly thought of chucking out all the clues he had, knowing we'd recognise them, and read them correctly!' said Fatty. 'Well! If Ern really did do that, he's cleverer than we ever thought him!'

He went back to the others, Buster trotting soberly at his heels. Buster always knew when his master was thinking hard, and never bothered him then.

Fatty told the others what he thought. They listened in silence. 'It was Bets' sudden idea that put me on to everything else,' said Fatty. 'Well – I've got to go and rescue Ern if I can – and perhaps I can solve this mystery at the same time! I'll go tonight.'

'Oh Fatty – don't do that!' begged Bets. 'Can't you ring up Inspector Jenks and tell him all you've said to us?'

'No,' said Fatty. 'Because I might be absolutely wrong about everything! Ern *might* be hiding in an old barn somewhere, sulking, to give Mr Goon a fright. And what do we really know of this other mystery? Hardly anything! Not as much as Old Clear-Orf knows of the imaginary one!'

'We'll come with you then, Fatty, if you're going tonight,' said Larry.

'You can't. You're forbidden,' said Fatty. 'In any case, I wouldn't let the girls come.'

'But we're not going to solve a mystery – we're going to rescue Ern,' protested Pip. 'That's quite different.'

'I'm going by myself,' said Fatty. 'I shall take a rope-ladder to get over the wall – and sacks to put on those spikes at the top so that I can climb over easily. Then – aha – there'll be dark dire deeds, as Ern would say!'

'Oh *don't*,' said Bets, with a shiver. 'I wish you wouldn't go, Fatty. Please don't!'

'Well, I feel rather bad about Ern,' said Fatty seriously. 'I feel as if he's had very bad luck all round – what with us pulling his leg – and Mr Goon scolding him for what he hadn't done – and then getting kidnapped because I once disguised myself as Ern. It's up to me to do *something*. I really *must* go, Bets, old thing.'

'I suppose you must,' said Bets, with a sigh.

They hunted for the rope-ladder, which was at last discovered on a shelf, neatly rolled up. Then they found sacks. Larry examined Fatty's torch to make sure the battery was all right. Bets slipped a bar of chocolate into his pocket. They all felt rather solemn, somehow, as if Fatty was going on a long, long journey!

'I'll start about half past eight, after I've had dinner with my Mummy and Daddy,' said Fatty.

They are going out to a bridge party afterwards, so I shall be able to slip out easily without anyone knowing.'

'Half past eight?' said Larry and Pip together. 'Sure you'll start then?'

'Yes. The moon won't be up. I shan't be seen at

all,' said Fatty. 'I shall take the same path over the field by the stream as we did before. Sorry you can't come with me, Pip and Larry.'

They looked at him solemnly. 'Yes,' said Pip. 'Spitty! Well – good luck, Fatty!'

21. INTO THE HEART OF THE MYSTERY

Fatty set out after dinner that night, at exactly half past eight. He had with him the rope-ladder and the sacks. Buster was left at home, whining and scratching at the shed door. He was very angry that Fatty should have left him behind.

Fatty made his way to the little bridge across the Bourne. He then walked cautiously along the frosty bank of the stream. Two shadowy figures came out from behind a tree and followed him quietly.

Fatty's sharp ears caught the soft crunch-crunch somewhere behind him. He stopped at once. He stiffened when he heard the footsteps coming quietly nearer. He saw the dim outline of a tree nearby and slipped behind it.

The footsteps drew nearer. He heard whispers. Two people then. Were they after him? What were they doing in the fields at that time of night?

Just as they passed, Fatty's sharp ears caught one

word in the whispered conversation. 'Buster . . .'

He grinned. He knew who it was following him now. It was Larry and Pip! They weren't going to be left out, whether they had been forbidden or not! Good old Larry and Pip!

He tiptoed after them. They soon stopped, not being able to hear Fatty in front of them any more. He spoke in a mournful voice just near them.

'Beware! Beware!'

Larry and Pip jumped violently. Then Pip stretched out his hand and touched Fatty. 'Fatty! It's you! Idiot! You did make us jump!'

'We *had* to come, Fatty,' said Larry. 'We couldn't let you go alone. We've decided that, mystery or not, we're all in it!'

Fatty gave Larry's arm a squeeze. 'Nice of you. Glad of your company, of course. Come on.'

They went on together, the three of them. After some time they came to where the narrow cart-track to Harry's Folly ran near to the stream. They left the bank and went into the little lane. They walked on steadily and silently in the darkness till they came to the iron gates. They were shut, of course. A light shone in the lodge nearby.

'We won't get over the wall here,' said Fatty. 'I don't think there *are* any dogs belonging to the lodge-keeper, but you never know. We'll walk round the wall a bit and choose a place some way off.'

They walked round the high wall. The sky was clearing now, and there was a fading starlight which helped them to see things better.

'This will do,' said Fatty. He hunted about and found a heavy stone. He tied it to the end of a rope he had which, in its turn, was fastened to the top of the rope-ladder.

'Help me chuck this stone over the wall,' said Fatty to Larry. The two boys took the stone between them. 'One, two, three, go!' said Fatty, and they heaved the stone up as hard as they could. It rose up and went neatly over the wall, dragging its short tail of rope behind it.

As the stone fell heavily to the ground on the other side, the rope-ladder was pulled up the wall by the rope attached to the falling stone. It rose up and stayed hanging on the wall. Fatty gave it a tug.

'Just right! Part of it's over the other side – and one of the rungs has got firmly held by the spikes at the top. Pip, you're the lightest. Shin up to the top, and we'll chuck the sacks for you to put on the spikes. Then sit on them, and make the ladder fast for us. Larry and I are heavy.'

Pip was light. The ladder shifted a little as he went up, but held firmly enough. The others threw up the sacks to him. Pip arranged them on the top of the wall so that they lay like a cushion over the spikes, preventing them from using their sharp points.

Pip sat on the sacks, and made the ladder as firm as he could for the others. Fatty gave it a hard tug. Yes. It was all right.

He made Pip come down again. Then he himself went up, sat on the sacks, pulled up the rope-ladder so that half hung down one side the ground and half the other – made it fast so that it could not slip, and then went down the other side, into the grounds of Harry's Folly. The others followed, clambering up one side and down the other.

'Good!' said Fatty, in a whisper. 'Now, we'll find the house!'

They made their way through thick trees. Fatty marked them with white chalk as he passed, for he was a little afraid that without some guide he might not be able to find his way back to the rope-ladder

– and they *might* be in a hurry later on!

After quite a long walk, the old house loomed up before them in the starlight. It looked forbidding in the dark night. Pip pressed close to the others, rather scared.

There was not a light to be seen anywhere. Fatty could dimly make out great shutters bolted across the windows. Then they came to a long flight of stone steps. The boys went up them silently. They led to a nail-studded front door, also tightly closed. The mansion seemed completely and utterly deserted.

'Do you think Ern is hidden somewhere here?' whispered Larry, his mouth close to Fatty's ear.

'Yes,' whispered back Fatty. 'There's some mystery about this place – it's used for something it shouldn't be used for, I'm sure, though I don't know what. And I'm certain Ern is here some-where. Come on – we've still got a good way to go round the house.'

In the darkness, the house seemed really enormous. The walls were endless to the boys as they walked cautiously beside them. There was no light anywhere and no noise at all.

They came to the back of the old house. A pond

gleamed dully in the starlight, frozen over. Two big flights of steps led down to it.

'What an enormous place!' whispered Pip. 'I wonder what its history is.'

'Shhhhhh!' hissed Fatty, and they all stood like stone, pressing against one another. They had heard a noise – a very curious noise. It seemed to come from underground!

'What is it? It's like some great machine at work,' whispered Larry. 'Where is it?'

They went on round the house, and came to what must have been either stables or garages. These were also enormous. A small door stood open in one of the garages, for Fatty could hear it creaking a little as it swung in the cold night wind. He made his way to it, the others following.

'Come on. This door's open. Let's go into the garage,' whispered Fatty, and in they went. It was dark, and the boys could see nothing at all. The noise they had heard was now quite gone.

Fatty cautiously got out his torch and shone it quickly round. They saw a vast garage, with shadowy corners. In front of them was a smooth expanse of floor.

Then a most terrifying thing happened! The floor

in front of them suddenly made a noise, moved, and sank swiftly down out of sight, into darkness! Fatty was so tremendously amazed that he couldn't even switch off his torch! He just stood there with it still shining, and in its light the boys saw the floor sink away below them. Another foot or two and they would have gone with it into blackness, goodness knows where!

Fatty snapped off his torch. Larry gripped him in fright. 'Fatty. What's happened? Did you see the floor go?'

'Yes. It's a moveable floor, worked by machinery,' said Fatty. 'Gave me a scare to see it disappear like that though! It hasn't gone down for nothing. Let's hide behind these big barrels and see if the floor comes back again.'

They hid behind the barrels for some time, getting cold and chilled. Nothing happened. Fatty flicked his torch quickly on and off again. The floor was still gone! A vast empty hole yawned below.

Fatty cautiously went to the edge, put on his torch and tried to light up the depth of blackness below him. A noise warned him to get back into hiding. He ran for his barrel.

A light, first dim and then brighter, now came up from the hole where the great floor had been. Noises came up from below too. Then voices shouted. Then came a curious whining sound – and the floor came up again, fitting into place! It really did behave like a lift that was nothing but a floor.

On the floor were three cars. None had any headlights on, only sidelamps.

Low voices spoke.

'All ready? Five minutes between each of you. You know what to do. Go now, Kenton.'

The great garage doors now rolled silently back. The first car rolled off the floor and went quietly out of the garage. It disappeared down the drive. When it came to the gatekeeper's lodge, it switched its headlights on and off once and waited. Peters came out, opened the gates quickly, the car slid out, and the gates closed again.

Five minutes later, the three boys saw the second car go. Then after another five minutes the third one went. Then the garage doors were shut again, and the only man left in the garage whistled softly.

He went and stood on the floor, and waited. After a minute or two, the floor slid downwards again, leaving the same yawning hole as before. Then there was a dead silence and complete darkness.

'Larry! Pip! Are you there?' came Fatty's whisper. 'We must do something or other now. We'll have to get down underground, I think. That's apparently where everything goes on. Are you game to?'

'Yes,' said both in a whisper. Fatty switched on his torch in a corner and showed the others some strong coiled wire rope he had found, used for towing one car behind another.

'If we tie this to that beam, see – and let the rope drop down the hole – we can swarm down in one by one.'

It didn't take long to make the rope secure to the beam. The end was dropped into the hole by Pip. Then Fatty tested it. It held all right. He sat down on the floor and took hold of the rope.

'I'll wait for you at the rope's end,' he whispered. 'Follow me quickly.'

Down he went easily, as if he was performing on the ropes at school. Pip followed and then Larry. Soon they stood far down underground, in complete darkness. As they stood there, they heard a noise of whirring and clattering some way off and a faint light came from that direction. Fatty saw the outline of a wide passage, and went down it, the others keeping close by him.

They followed the wide passage, which wound round and round rather like an enormous spiral stairway. 'We're going down into the bowels of the earth!' whispered Larry. 'Whatever's this curious winding passage, Fatty?'

'It's where cars come up to go on to that automatic floor,' said Fatty. 'Or go down! Ah – here we are!'

From their dark corner, the boys now looked out into an enormous workshop. Machines whirred and clattered. There were cars everywhere! Two were being sprayed with blue cellulose paint. Another was being scraped. A fourth was almost in pieces. Others stood about with nobody working on them.

'What sort of place is this, Fatty?' asked Larry in a puzzled whisper.

'I'm not absolutely sure,' said Fatty. 'But I rather think it's a receiving place for stolen cars. They are brought here in the dark, put on the moving floor, taken down here and completely altered so that nobody would ever recognise them again. Then they are sent above-ground again at night – and I imagine sold for a colossal sum with faked logbooks!'

'Whew!' said Larry. 'I heard my father saying the other day that the police were completely baffled over the amount of stolen cars disappearing lately. I bet this is where they come to. My word, Fatty – what a find!'

22. A STRANGE NIGHT

'I say, Fatty, look – who's that coming down those stairs at the end?' said Pip suddenly. 'He must be the Boss. See the way the men straighten up and salute him.'

'It's Mr Holland!' said Fatty. 'Oho, Mr Holland, so this is your little hideout! You knew far more about Harry's Folly than you wanted to admit. What business he must do in stolen cars!'

'I wonder how many of the men in his garage at Marlow know about this?' said Pip.

'None of them, I should imagine,' said Fatty. 'He keeps those garages of his as a very nice cover for himself. But this is his real line. My word, Inspector Jenks would like to know about this little nest of cars!'

The men had evidently had some kind of order to knock off work for a meal or drink, for one by one they left their jobs and disappeared into a further room. Mr Holland went with them.

The workshop was deserted. 'Now's our chance,' whispered Fatty. 'We must scoot to those stairs over there – the ones Mr Holland came down – and go up them. It's our only chance of finding Ern.'

They ran quietly to the stairs, and were up them long before the men returned to the workshop. The stairway was spiral, like the ascending passageway to the place where the movable floor was. But this passageway was very narrow and much steeper. The boys panted a little as they went. At the top of the stairs was a wide landing. Doors opened off it. Another flight of steps led upwards.

'Weird place!' said Fatty. 'Must have been used in the past for something very hush-hush, as I said before. Something very secret must have been made down in that vast workshop – goodness knows what. Bombs perhaps!'

The boys looked round at all the closed doors, fearing that one might open suddenly and somebody come out and challenge them. Fatty looked up the next flight of steps. 'I suppose those lead to the ground floor of the mansion,' he said. 'Well – what shall we do? Try these doors, or go up the stairs?'

At that very moment there came a familiar sound – a rather forlorn, hollow cough.

'Ern!' said Pip at once. 'I'd know that cough anywhere. It's so like Mr Goon's. Ern is in one of these rooms!'

'That one, I think,' said Fatty and went quietly to a door opposite. He cautiously turned the handle – but the door would not open. Then Fatty saw that the door was bolted – and probably locked too – for the key was on his side of the door.

He unbolted the door carefully. He unlocked it. He pushed it open and looked in. Ern was lying on a bed, a pencil in his hand, his portry notebook beside him. He was muttering something to himself.

'Ern!' said Fatty.

Ern sat up so suddenly that his notebook flew to the floor. He gazed at the three boys in astonishment that changed to the utmost delight. He threw himself off the bed and ran to them. He flung his arms round Fatty.

'Fatty! I knew you'd come! I knew you'd follow the clues I threw out of the car. Fatty, the kidnappers got me! Oooh, I've had the most awful time trying to tell them I don't know anything at all. They keep saying I'm you, Fatty! They're all potty.'

'Sh!' said Fatty. 'Are you quite all right, Ern? They haven't hurt you, have they?'

'No,' said Ern. 'But they don't give me much food. And they said they'd starve me tomorrow if I don't answer their questions properly. But I don't know the answers. Fatty, let's go!'

'Larry – go to the door and keep watch,' ordered Fatty. 'Tell me at once if there's any sound of somebody coming up that spiral stairway. At once, mind!'

He turned back to Ern, who was now almost in tears with excitement. 'Listen Ern – can you do something really brave?'

'Coo! I don't know,' said Ern doubtfully.

'Well, listen,' said Fatty. 'We're right in the very middle of a great big mystery here – and I want to get to the police and tell them about it before the men are warned that somebody knows their secret. Now Ern – if we take you away with us tonight, the men will know their game is up, for they'll find you gone and know that someone has rescued you. So, will you stay here, locked up, all night long, in order to let the men think everything is all right – and wait till the police come in the morning?'

'I can't do that,' said Ern, almost crying. 'You don't know what it's like, to be a prisoner like this and not know what's going to happen to you. I can't even think of any portry.'

'Aren't you brave enough to do this one thing?' said Fatty sadly. 'I did want to think well of you, Ern.'

Ern stared at Fatty, who looked back at him solemnly.

'All right,' said Ern. 'I'll do it, see! I'll do it for *you*, Fatty, because you're a wonder, you are! But I don't feel brave about it. I feel all of a tremble.'

'When you feel afraid to do a thing and yet do it, that's *real* bravery,' said Fatty. 'You're a hero, Ern!'

Ern was so chuffed at these words that he now felt he would have stayed locked up for a week if necessary! He beamed at Fatty.

'Did Bets tell you about the wonderful pome I wrote in my sleep?' he asked anxiously. 'You should see it, Fatty. Lovaduck, I feel so proud when I remember it. It's the best pome I ever wrote. I don't know when I've felt so pleased about anything. I feel reel proud of myself.'

Now was the time for Fatty to confess to Ern that he had played a trick on him and written out the poem in Ern's own handwriting – but Fatty, looking at Ern's proud face, simply hadn't the heart to tell him. Ern would be so bitterly disappointed! Let him think it was his own poem, if he was so proud of it. Fatty felt so embarrassed about the whole thing that he almost blushed. Whatever had possessed him to play such an idiotic trick on Ern?

'Sssssst!' suddenly came warningly from Larry and Pip. Fatty gave Ern a pat on the back and murmured, 'Good fellow, see you tomorrow!' He melted out of the room, closed, locked, and bolted the door in an amazingly deft and silent way, and then pulled Larry and Pip up the further flight of stairs.

They had no sooner got up than Mr Holland appeared at the top of the spiral stairway. He went into one of the rooms. The three boys did not dare go down again.

'Better go on up to the top of these stairs and see where we are,' whispered Fatty. So up they went. They soon found themselves on the ground floor of the great mansion. Fatty flicked on his torch. The boys shivered.

Cobwebs hung everywhere. Dust rose from the floor as they trod over it. A musty, sour smell hung over everything.

Fatty looked at his watch. 'Do you know it's almost one o'clock!' he said, his whisper echoing round the room mysteriously. 'Let's get out of here somehow and go and give the warning to Inspector Jenks.'

But they could not get out! Shutters closed the windows on the outside, so even if the boys could have unfastened a window, they could not have undone the shutters. Every outside door they tried was locked, but without a key! It was just like a nightmare, wandering through the dark, dusty house, unable to get out anywhere.

'This is frightful,' said Fatty at last. 'I've never felt so completely done in my life. There's nowhere we can get out at all!'

'Well – we shall have to see if we can go back the way we came,' said Larry. 'We can't go through that enormous workshop while the men are at work there. We'll have to wait till they go for a meal again. Come on, let's go down the stairs to Ern's landing and see if anyone is there.'

They went silently down. The landing was empty. No sound came from Ern's room. He was not asleep though. He was awake, feeling very solemn and exultant. He was being a hero, being really brave for

Fatty's sake. Ern felt thrilled – and hoped intensely that Mr Holland wouldn't come and badger him again with questions he couldn't answer. Suppose he asked him if any of the others had been there that night? Ern lost himself in dreadful thoughts of what might happen to him if Mr Holland tried to worm a lot of things out of him, thinking Ern was hiding something from him. He felt anything but a hero then.

The boys crept down the spiral stairway. Work was in full swing again in the workshop. Mr Holland stood with his hands in his pockets talking to another man. Nobody could see the boys because they were in such a dark corner.

For two hours the tired boys watched. Then Pip suddenly fell asleep on the stairway, his head rolling on Fatty's shoulder.

'We'll take turns at watching,' said Fatty. 'You sleep too, Larry. I'll wake you if anyone comes this way.'

So two of them slept and Fatty kept watch. At half past three he awoke Larry, who kept watch while he slept. Still the work in the great place below them went on at full speed. Half past five came and Pip was awakened and told to keep watch. He was fresh after his four hours' sleep and looked with interest at everything going on. Nobody came near their corner.

It seemed as if there would be no chance at all of getting out. When Fatty awoke suddenly at seven o'clock, he felt worried. Time was getting on. They couldn't stay here much longer.

A big lorry was suddenly backed almost into their corner. The boys all retired a little way up the stairway in a hurry. Then an idea came to Fatty.

'That lorry's going out! It seems quite finished. If we get into the back, we might slip out with the lorry unseen. We've got to get out *somehow*!'

The others were quite willing. When the man who had backed the lorry into their corner had got down to speak to Mr Holland a little way off, the three boys climbed quietly into the back of the lorry. To their relief, there was a partition between the driver's cabin and the back of the van, so that nobody could see them from the driver's seat. There were some old papers and sacks in the lorry. The boys covered themselves with these.

The man came back to the lorry. He started up the engine. So did two drivers of other cars. They were ready to go out. They had come in a week or two before – stolen, all of them – now they had been repainted, touched up, altered beyond even the owner's recognition – and were ready to go out and be sold again, with false logbooks.

The lorry went slowly up the winding stone passage, up and up and up, following the other cars. They came to the moveable floor and ran on to it. A minute's wait and the floor went upwards like a lift!

One by one, at five minute intervals, the cars ran silently out of the garage. In the last one, the lorry, lay the three hidden boys. The lorry driver flashed his headlights on and off once, and waited for the gates to open at the end of the drive. In that minute, the three boys slipped out of the lorry!

They waited in the shadow of the trees till the gates were closed and everything was quiet. Then they went to the wall. 'Have to feel our way round till we come to the ladder,' whispered Fatty. 'Fat lot of good my marking the trees as I did. Come on! We'll soon find the ladder – and then up we'll go and away home.'

23. INSPECTOR JENKS
TAKES OVER

Meantime Mr Goon had been sitting up all night long, expecting and hoping the telephone would ring to say that Fatty had found Ern.

But it didn't ring until eight o'clock the next morning, when an anxious Mrs Hilton telephoned to say that Pip was missing! He hadn't been home all night. Bets was in a dreadful state of worry and had told her mother such extraordinary things that nobody could make anything of them.

Then Larry and Daisy's father rang. Larry was missing! They couldn't get anything out of Daisy at all except that Fatty was in charge and everything was all right.

'Daisy says that Fatty has gone out to solve a mystery, but that Larry and Pip have gone to rescue your nephew. Mr Goon, do you know anything about this at all?'

Well, Mr Goon did. But what he knew was going

to be very difficult to explain to angry and alarmed parents. He hummed and hawed, and then, at a banging on his door, hurriedly put down the receiver to answer the door, hoping against hope that it was Fatty with good news.

But it wasn't. It was Mr Trotteville! Fatty was missing – hadn't been in bed all night! Mr Trotteville had tried to ring up Mr Goon repeatedly but his telephone appeared to be engaged every time. Did Mr Goon know anything about where Fatty had gone?

What with Ern being gone for two days and now three more boys missing, Mr Goon began to feel he really couldn't stand any more. He telephoned the Inspector.

'Sir, I'm sorry to worry you so early in the morning – but there's all kinds of things happening here, sir, and I was wondering if you could come over,' said the agitated voice of Mr Goon.

'What sort of things, Goon?' asked the Inspector. 'Chimneys on fire or lost dogs or something? Can't you manage them yourself?'

'No, sir. Yes, sir. I mean, sir, it's nothing like that at all, sir,' said Mr Goon desperately. 'My nephew's disappeared, sir – and Frederick Trotteville went to find him – and now he's gone too, sir, and so have Larry and Pip. I don't know if it's the robbers or the kidnappers who have taken them, sir.'

The Inspector listened to this astounding information in surprise. 'I'll be right over, Goon,' he said, and hung up the receiver. He ordered his shining black car, got in and drove over to Peterswood, wondering what Frederick Trotteville was up to now. Inspector Jenks had a feeling that if he could put his finger on Frederick Trotteville, he would soon get to the bottom of everything.

He drove to Mr Goon's house and found him in a state of collapse. 'Oh, sir, I'm so glad you've come,' stuttered Mr Goon, leading the Inspector by mistake into the kitchen and then out again into the sitting-room.

'Pull yourself together, Goon,' said the Inspector severely. 'What's happened, man?'

'Well, it all began when my young nephew, Ern, came to stay with me,' began Mr Goon. 'I warned the others, sir, not to lead him into no mysteries – you know what that young Frederick Trotteville is, sir, for getting into trouble – and the first thing I know is that there's a mystery up on Christmas Hill, sir – two gangs there – one robbers and one kidnappers.'

'Most extraordinary, Goon,' said the Inspector. 'Go on.'

'Well, sir, I went up to inspect one night – and sure enough there were lights flashing by the hundred all round me – red, blue and green, sir – a most amazing sight.'

'Quite a firework show!' said the Inspector.

'Then, sir, there were awful noises – like cows bellowing, sir, and hens clucking, and cats mewing and – and, well, the most peculiar noises you ever heard, sir.'

The Inspector eyed Mr Goon sharply. He had a sort of feeling that if cows suddenly mooed on deserted hills, and hens clucked and cats mewed, there might possibly be some boy there having a fine old joke with Mr Goon. And that boy's name would be Fatty.

'Then, sir,' said Mr Goon, warming up, 'a great hefty giant of a man flung himself on me, sir – got me right down on my face, he did. He hit me and almost knocked me out. I had to fight for my life, sir. But I fought him off, and gave him a fearful trouncing. He'll bear the marks to his dying day.'

'And you caught him, handcuffed him, and brought him back with you,' suggested the Inspector.

'No, sir. He got away,' said Mr Goon sadly. 'Well, then sir, I heard as how a robbery had been committed and the loot, sir, was to be hidden in the old mill.'

'And how did you hear that?' asked the Inspector with interest. 'And why not inform me?'

'I heard it from my young nephew, sir,' said Mr Goon. 'He got it from Frederick.'

'I see,' said the Inspector, beginning to understand quite a lot of things. That scamp of a Fatty! He had led poor Mr Goon properly astray this time. Inspector Jenks regretfully decided that he would have to give Fatty a good ticking-off.

'Then, sir, my nephew disappeared. He just went out and never came back. Two days ago that was.'

The Inspector asked the question that Mr Goon had been dreading.

'Was the boy in any trouble?'

'Well – a bit,' admitted Mr Goon. 'He – er – he wrote an extremely rude pome about me, sir – and I corrected him.'

'In what way?' asked the Inspector.

'I just gave him a severe scolding, sir,' said Mr Goon. 'But I'm sure that's not what made him run away, sir – if he has run away. He's very fond of me, sir, and he's my favourite nephew.'

'H'm,' said the Inspector, doubting all this very much. 'What next?'

'Well, sir, Frederick told me he thought he knew where Ern was, and if I'd wait till night, he'd probably bring him back again. So I waited up all last night, sir, but Frederick didn't come back – and now all the parents of those kids have rung up or come to see me to complain that their boys are missing!'

'This sounds rather serious to me,' said the Inspector. 'Are you sure you've told me everything, Goon?'

'Well – everything that's any use,' said Mr Goon hastily. 'I went up after the loot, sir, but I couldn't find it.'

'I wonder where in the world those four boys are!' said Inspector Jenks. 'I can't quite see where to begin looking for them. Or what to do. Where *can* they be?'

At that very moment, three of the boys were staggering home! They had found their rope-ladder, climbed up over the wall, and dropped down the other side. They had lost their way, and wandered about for some time before they got back to the cart-track they knew. They were so tired that they hardly knew what they were doing.

By now it was getting light. Thankfully Fatty, Larry, and Pip stumbled along the banks of the little stream. What miles it seemed! At last they came to the bridge and made their way into the village.

'Better go to Mr Goon first and tell him Ern's all right,' said Fatty. 'I'll telephone the Inspector from there. Gosh, I'm tired!'

To the Inspector's astonishment, as he stood looking out of the window, he suddenly saw Fatty, Larry and Pip walking like very tired old men up the street.

'Look, Goon!' he said. 'Here are three of them. But no Ern!'

Mr Goon groaned dismally. The three boys walked up his front path and knocked at the door. Fatty gasped with surprise and pleasure when the Inspector opened the door to him. 'Oh sir! This is lovely! You're just the person I wanted to see,' he said, and shook hands warmly.

'You're not fit to stand, any of you,' said the

Inspector, looking at the dirty, tired boys. 'Goon, put on some milk for cocoa for these three. They could do with something. Then ring up their parents and tell them they are safe. Get on with it, now!'

Mr Goon hurried to do as he was told. No Ern! Oh, what had happened to him? He felt that if only Ern would come back he would never ever again say a cross word to him. Never!

Fatty and the others sank into chairs. Pip's eyes began to close.

'I'll take you all back in my car,' said the Inspector. 'You can tell me your story later. I already know about this, er – rather incredible mystery on Christmas Hill, Frederick – with flashing lights, mysterious noises, and the rest.'

'Oh that!' said Fatty. 'That's nothing, sir. That wasn't a mystery at all.'

'So I gathered,' said the Inspector. 'Ah, here is the cocoa. Thanks, Goon. Now ring up those boys' parents will you?'

'Sir, may I ask just one question first?' pleaded Mr Goon. 'It's about Ern. Is he all right?'

'Oh, Ern. Yes, he's quite all right as far as I know,'

said Fatty, taking a deep drink of the cocoa. 'Gosh, I've burnt my mouth.'

'Drink up the cocoa, and then get into my car,' said Inspector Jenks, alarmed at the pale, worn-out faces of the three boys. Pip was fast asleep.

'Good gracious, sir! I've got a story that will keep you busy for the rest of the day!' said Fatty, feeling better for the cocoa. He took another drink.

'Don't let Mr Goon telephone our parents, sir,' he said. 'You'll want the phone yourself in another couple of minutes! I've got a first class mystery for you, sir! All ready to hand to you on a plate!'

24. A NEAT MYSTERY
– AND A NEAT ENDING!

Mr Goon came into the room, his eyes bulging. 'What do you mean? A first class mystery! Haven't you just said that mystery up on Christmas Hill wasn't one at all? And what about those lights then, and those noises, and that giant of a fellow that nearly killed me? What about *them*?'

'Oh those!' said Fatty. 'Larry and Pip flashed the lights. I made the noises. And I pounced on you in the ditch, thinking you were Ern.'

Mr Goon collapsed like a pricked balloon. 'Frederick must have been very strong if he seemed like a giant to you,' said the Inspector to Mr Goon with a laugh.

'And the gangs, of course, were all made up, just to play a trick on Ern,' said Fatty. 'It wasn't our fault if Mr Goon believed everything too. We didn't think he'd be as silly as Ern.'

Mr Goon went red to the ears, but he said nothing.

'We threw down a lot of clues for Ern,' said Fatty,

'and made a story up about some loot that was hidden in the old mill. We meant Ern to go and look, but instead of that, poor Ern got a scolding and was locked in his bedroom – and Mr Goon went to find the loot instead. But it wasn't there, of course.'

Mr Goon wanted to sink down through the floor but he couldn't. He sat there looking very unhappy indeed. That pestering boy!

'Well, Inspector, what began the *real* mystery was this,' said Fatty, taking another drink. 'Ern went off to Christmas Hill, as he thought – but he lost his way, and saw one or two strange things over at Bourne Wood. And that set us thinking.'

'Go on,' said the Inspector. 'So you did a bit of detecting?'

'Yes sir,' said Fatty modestly. 'We soon knew there was something fishy going on at Harry's Folly, sir – the building in the middle of Bourne Wood. We went to see the caretaker – the man at the lodge called Mr Peters – and we made a few inquiries about a man called Mr Holland, who seemed a pretty strange customer . . .'

'*Holland*?' said the Inspector, sitting up straight. 'What do you know about him?'

'Quite a lot now,' said Fatty, with a grin. 'Why, do you know him too, sir?'

'We've been suspicious of him for a long time,' said the Inspector. 'But there was never anything we could put our finger on. Lived quietly with an old aunt in Peterswood, gave to the churches around – all that kind of thing – and yet his name cropped up here and there in peculiar circumstances. Well – go on . . .'

'I disguised myself as Ern one day and went over to Mr Holland's garage to make inquiries – and he must have recognised my name, sir – as being – er – well, a bit of a detective, sir – and so, when he saw *Ern* wandering around alone in a lonely lane, he kidnapped him – thinking he was me, sir.'

'I see,' said the Inspector. Mr Goon sat and looked as if he really couldn't believe his ears!

'Ern was clever, sir,' said Fatty. 'He threw a whole lot of clues out of the car – pretending he was feeling sick, or something, I should think – and Mr Goon here picked them up and gave them to me.'

Mr Goon gulped. The Inspector looked at him. 'Very kind of Goon. I suppose he knew you would make good use of them.'

'Yes sir. Actually he thought we'd put the clues there ourselves to fool him. As if we'd do a thing like that, sir!'

'Well, I wouldn't put it past you,' said the Inspector. 'But go on. We're wasting time.'

'I did a bit of deduction, sir, and thought Ern must have been kidnapped and was probably taken to Harry's Folly. So Larry and Pip and I set off to rescue him last night. We got in, sir, rope-ladder and all that – and found the house deserted. But in the garage, sir – my word!'

Goon and the Inspector were listening hard now. Pip was still fast asleep in his chair.

'There was a moveable floor there, sir, that sank right down. It takes cars. They go down on it like a lift and then run slowly down a winding passage deep underground. And there's a workshop there, sir – with heaps of cars being repainted and done over . . .'

The Inspector whistled. 'My word! So *that's* where it is! We've been looking for that workshop for a long long time, Frederick. You remember, Goon, I reported it to you two years ago and asked you to keep a lookout in your district, as we had information it was here somewhere. And there it was, all the time, right under your nose! Well done, Frederick, my boy!'

'We found Ern, sir, and he said he'd stay in his locked room all night long, so that his escape wouldn't raise the alarm. It would give us a chance to get back here and warn you, sir, so that perhaps you could catch the whole gang at work.'

'Very brave of the boy,' said the Inspector approvingly. 'Good work! I hope you agree with me, Goon?'

'Yes, sir,' mumbled Goon, marvelling at the idea of Ern appearing suddenly as a hero.

'So we left him there, and had a hard job getting out unseen,' said Fatty. 'Went out in one of their own lorries in the end! And here we are!'

'A very fine job of work, Frederick,' said the Inspector, getting up. 'And now, as you so wisely said, I shall have to have the use of the phone for a few minutes.'

Inspector Jenks went to the telephone and dialled rapidly. Larry and Fatty listened raptly. Pip still slept peacefully on. Mr Goon looked gloomily at his hands. Always that boy came out on top. And Ern a hero, too! It wasn't possible that anyone could have such bad luck as Mr Goon!

Inspector Jenks spoke rapidly and to the point. Fatty listened in glee. Six police cars! Whew, what a round-up! He dug Larry in the ribs and they both grinned at one another.

The Inspector stopped phoning. 'Now I'm going to take you all home,' he said. 'It will be a few minutes before the police cars come along. Wake Pip up, and we'll get cracking.'

'Look here, Inspector, I'm going with you to Harry's Folly, aren't I?' said Fatty, in alarm. 'You wouldn't be so mean as to leave me out at the end of it, would you? After all, I've done all the dirty work so far, and so have Larry and Pip.'

'All right. You can come with me if you want to – in *my* car,' said the Inspector. 'But I may as well tell you that you won't be in the thick of it – only a witness! Now do wake that boy up and bring him along.'

Larry and Fatty half-carried the sleepy Pip to the Inspector's car. Then, with a roar, the engine started up and the powerful car sprang forward. Pip was deposited at his house with a few words of explanation. He sat down in a chair and went off to sleep again, in spite of Bets' frantic questions.

Then to Larry's home, where poor Larry was ordered to stay behind. Then to Fatty's own home, where a half-mad Buster hurled himself at Fatty as if he had been away for a year.

'Frederick is safe,' said the Inspector to Fatty's surprised parents. 'Bit of a marvel, as usual. Do you mind if I borrow him for a time? All news when I see you again.'

And Fatty was whipped away again in the car, with a very happy Buster on his knee, licking the underneath of his master's chin till it dripped.

Six other police cars joined them, and went slowly along the narrow cart-track to Harry's Folly. Peters, the gatekeeper, was terrified when he saw the posse of blue-coated figures at the gate. He opened it without a word, and was captured immediately, pale and trembling, looking quite different from the surly, bad-tempered fellow the five children had encountered some days before.

Fatty remained behind with the Inspector in his car, shaking with excitement. What was happening?

Plenty was happening. The raid was a complete

and utter surprise. Every man down below in the workshop was rounded up – and Mr Holland was discovered asleep in one of the bedrooms near Ern's!

Ern was not asleep. He was waiting and waiting. He didn't feel he could be a hero much longer. He was so terribly hungry, for one thing!

He was so glad to see Fatty, when he was led to the car by one of the policemen, that he could hardly keep from hugging him.

'So this is Ern,' said the Inspector, and to the boy's enormous delight and surprise, he shook hands with him very warmly. 'Quite a hero, I hear – and a bit of a poet too. I must read that poem you wrote about your uncle, Ern. I'm sure it's very very good.'

Ern blushed. 'Oh, sir. Thank you, sir! I couldn't show it to you, sir. My uncle wouldn't like me to.'

The Inspector's car moved off, with the others following in a close line. 'A very good haul, Frederick,' said Inspector Jenks. 'A neat little mystery and a neat ending. Thanks very much, my boy. Make haste and grow up! I want a right-hand man, you know!'

Fatty went red with pleasure, 'Right, sir, I'll do my best to grow up as soon as I can!'

They arrived at Mr Goon's. Ern got out. He looked miserable all of a sudden.

'Come on in, Ern,' said the Inspector, pulling him indoors. 'Goon! Here's Ern back again. Quite a hero! And I hear he's written a very fine poem about you. Shall we hear it?'

'Well . . .' said Mr Goon, going scarlet, 'it's, it's not very *polite*, sir . . .'

'It's all right, Uncle, I won't read it,' said Ern, taking pity on his uncle. 'I'll tear it up, see?'

'You're a good boy, Ern,' said Mr Goon. 'I'm really glad to see you back. I've got some bacon and eggs ready to cook for you. Like that?'

'Lovaduck!' said Ern, his face beaming. 'I could eat a horse. I'm that hungry.'

'Good-bye Ern,' said Fatty. 'See you later.'

He drove off with the Inspector, who was taking him home to report on the exciting happenings. 'That poem of Ern's,' said the Inspector, neatly turning in at Fatty's drive. 'I'm sorry I didn't have the pleasure of reading it, after all.'

'Yes,' said Fatty yawning. 'Spitty.'

'What?' said the Inspector in surprise.

'Spitty,' said Fatty. 'Swatlsaid.' He slumped down

against the Inspector's arm, and his eyes closed. He was fast asleep!

The Inspector left him there asleep, and went in to have a talk with Fatty's parents. What he said about Fatty should have made both his ears burn! But they didn't, because Fatty was lost in dreams that came crowding into his mind, thick and fast.

Flashing lights – moveable floors – Christmas Hill – dark dire deeds – clues in plenty – spiral stairways – a dark dark house – and there was Ern, crowned with laurel leaves, a hero! He was just going to recite a marvellous poem.

'Lovaduck!' said Fatty, and woke up.